D1159865

The
Advent
of
Frederick
Giles

Novels by
Josiah Bunting III

THE LIONHEADS

THE ADVENT OF FREDERICK GILES

The Advent of Frederick Giles

Josiah Bunting III

LITTLE, BROWN AND COMPANY — BOSTON — TORONTO

109133

FIRST EDITION

T 04/74

Library of Congress Cataloging in Publication Data

Bunting, Josiah.
    A ceremony of lessons.

    I. Title.
PZ4.B9383Ce [PS3552.U48]   813'.5'4   73-18340
ISBN 0-316-11490-1

Published simultaneously in Canada
by Little, Brown & Company (Canada) Limited

PRINTED IN THE UNITED STATES OF AMERICA

To My Parents
to Edwin Seaver
and
to Tom, Marcella, and Paul

. . . and in our enemies we have a particularly sharp eye for our own faults in an exaggerated form. All that Macaulay says of Brougham might be said, by a hostile critic, of Macaulay himself.

D. H. Fraser
"Macaulay's Style as an Essayist"

ONE

Giles

1

The last time we went to England was two years ago this winter. There were four of us, Marjorie and I and two of our children. We flew over and back and were there about two weeks, dividing our time between London, where I worked, and a town in Surrey where we all stayed. This was called Lawnsmere.

Almost all my memories of that visit are sad or unpleasant ones, and lately, and without wanting to, I have begun thinking about it often. Two things especially bring it to mind. One of them is flying, and in my business I'm flying almost constantly these days. The other is any music identifiably English: the orchestral music of Delius or Elgar, for example, or any of that rich stock of native English Christmas carols recorded by the choir at King's College Chapel in Cambridge. Our visit, you see, happened to coincide with the Christmas holidays. And I might also mention that I took an undistinguished degree at Cambridge ten years ago.

So business flights and English music evoke memories of that trip, arouse and release them in great bitter flood. It's something like walking along a deserted beach in the wintertime and being reminded of high summer with its resort fragrances and excited shrieks of children leaping in the surf. And isolated details like these work on my mind like an undertow, always drawing me irresistibly back and away from them: far enough away that, recessed, they merge and lose themselves in a larger,

3

grander prospect, a whole much less memorable and forlorn than any of its details.

It's the same with my recollection of our trip, except that the details still stand out, adamantly redefining themselves. They grow separately sharper, more vivid and more painful, and now it is only by the most determined act of will that I can force myself to see our visit in its real perspective; that I can make myself realize those two weeks in England didn't really do our marriage any harm, and that things between Marjorie and me are not much different now from what they were before we went to Lawnsmere.

We flew over through a deep Atlantic night, the air cold enough to singe you to dust if you'd been out in it. I remember the stars seeming to float and tumble all around us, and thinking there must still be a few proud liners on the ocean below — ships, I imagined, full of lovers and revelers, men and women in staterooms thick with perfume and the febrile heat of sex, and I was desperately sorry we weren't on one of them. The 747 seemed to sail without thrust, as though where its course diverged from the coast it had begun to sail, had been cast out like a discus from the Grand Banks to the North of Europe. We sailed and coasted in the slipstream, and I recall expecting that the plane would have to buck and fight its way over the ocean like the great ships going along underneath us. But it sailed and glided easily, on and on...

I thought then of the old *Berengaria* my mother had sailed on years before she knew my father, a ship she had described for me once when I was a boy, a ship with palms in its foyers and along the wide marble esplanade giving onto its grand ballroom. I imagined sleek unctuous men showing their profiles to advantage as they descended slowly to the dancing, and now, flying to England, I thought of Eddy Duchin and Marjorie Oelrichs, especially of Duchin and the simple eloquence of his playing and the songs my mother loved: "Long Ago and Far Away," and "It's All Right with Me."

I forgot the *Berengaria* and Eddy Duchin. Then I remembered being home from Lawrenceville ten years after my father was killed. The Jerome Kern and Cole Porter songs were still being played, and we kept going most of the night in the St. Regis, and girls were being presented and slipping out from under their quavering curtsies, trying frantically to redeem themselves, smiling their starchy grins like *kouroi*, scuttling away from some Grand Stuffed-Shirt Master of Frolics, pumping their little elbows like pistons. We would dance energetic foxtrots with them and finally would take them back to our parents' apartments and make ourselves jittery with brandy. Inevitably I would wind up wrestling with them on a sofa. "Go in the bathroom and feel better," one of them said to me once.

But it was 1971 now. There was a new kind of social currency in the world. The button-down shirt had long since penetrated to Egg Harbor, N.J., and the old malarkey I could live with was gone, all of it succeeded by woefully debased and banal new rates of exchange. In college we had listened to Chubby Checker and Fats Domino ("Mark, can you speak to Mr. Domino and ask him to play more quietly?") and then we had our generation's quota of assassinations, I guessed, and our nasty long little war; we had our Marcuses and when we were arriving at Kennedy that night I saw Representative

McCloskey was going to do New Hampshire in a car, a rented mid-size.

I didn't care whether the world I had grown up in had vanished, any more than I cared, or mused about, this odd assembly of memories and opinions. I was somewhat drunk, I remember. Marjorie and the children seemed to sleep, my daughter in her mother's arms and my son twisted over onto my lap from the adjoining seat. I felt terribly protective towards them then, and a little smug, I think, that I felt this way.

The plane was almost empty; no hairy-melon half-heads stuck up between me and Mr. George C. Scott on the screen three or four rows in front of us. Here and there narrow cylinders of light, smoke curling through them, distinguished the faces of nervous fliers reading their way to London, faces drawn and gelid in the milky illumination, faces peering down at novels, at *Barron's* or at *Newsweek*. The aisles remained empty. Abruptly George C. Scott disappeared from the screen, and I found myself fiddling at the dial on the armrest of my seat until it clicked at the classical setting and summoned up some violent disordered piano concerto through the plastic stethoscope I had not taken out before, a cascade roaring in on me like a wild winter's night rasping through an open door. "Classical," you understand, means "Romantic" to the international airlines: a writhing Liszt étude or the syrup of the Mendelssohn Violin Concerto or even, as earlier that night, an 1812 Overture with cannon rented from Headquarters, British Rhine Army. Just behind the throw-up bag hung a folder giving details.

Scott reappeared, as cold and self-possessed as Haydn. He was engaged in tightening his belt around the hollow of his left arm, between his bicep and shoulder. Smoke purled from a cigarette at his lips into those equine nostrils of his, which of course bothered him not at all, while his right hand expertly manipulated a syringe into position over a vein in the crook of his arm. He was preparing to shoot up with what I gathered was some sort of toxic fluid. He was going to kill himself, I found out later, because he had been unable to achieve an erection. But suddenly a woman was bursting onto the honeycombed screen from the aisle of the 747 and this was the end of the machinations with belt and syringe, a great disappointment to anyone absorbed in movies about professionals subverting their expertise to misbegotten ends. In any case the drinks I had had were slowly doing their work; I was drifting into sleep, going off with my hand on my son's hair, resolving he should lift weights in the cellar and never play in the Little League.

I dozed, the plane sagged, I woke to the muted crackle of static. Captain Faunce-Hugh was telling us that our descent would soon begin, and that we were now over Bell-fahst.

My wife and I adore the English, as you will see, but the English had their Vietnam too. I was moved to ask the stewardess whether one could make out the flashes of four-deuce mortars bursting thirty thousand feet below — it was still more black than gray outside — and she replied crisply, obviously unwilling to be drawn, "We're at twenty thousand feet, actually, we've begun our descent."

Marjorie was not amused by this. How would I like it, she wondered, if I picked up an English hitchhiker on the Merritt Parkway and he gave me static about Vietnam? But I didn't care. The situations aren't the same, I told her, and she turned away.

I remember sliding out of a cloudbank towards Heathrow Airport and making out the patterned rectilinear landscape going along under us. I remember being suddenly conscious that I was happier than I had ever been before: happy with the gentle slipping towards the earth, and with the prospect of two or three weeks in England, of seeing friends I had made years ago at Cambridge, and of visiting one of my wife's kinsmen — an uncle on her mother's side who had fought in the Western Desert under the doughty O'Connor and with whom I shared a maturing friendship because I had served in the Eastern Jungle under the doughty Westmoreland. "Yet her people remained steadfast and unflinching," said Edward R. Murrow of that time, Uncle Orme Goderich's wartime; none more than Orme, who had been captured at what he called the "base of an escarpment," and had had to endure almost five years of prison.

We were going to stay near him, in Surrey, but there would be time for trips elsewhere, to places I had missed when I lived in Cambridge, but which now — because of research commitments — might quite plausibly have to be visited. Marjorie and the children would remain in a hotel in Surrey and I would take the train up to London each morning to work at the Record Office or in the Army Museum in Chelsea. She would be near Orme, but not so near that the children would get on his nerves, and I would get in each night at seven, and we would sit in the pub drinking with the locals.

The plane had landed under a weak winter sun and stopped on the tarmac. We were on the top deck of the airport bus and my son was throwing up on my chesterfield while my daughter chirped brightly at a tiny Pakistani child across the aisle. We were driven slowly through Chelsea to the BOAC terminal; from there in a cab to Waterloo Station; and finally we were in a train going briskly along, briskly and efficiently along about its business like anything English on a Tuesday morning, going along to Lawnsmere in Surrey while we ate eggs and bacon and waited for the country to open up below Esher.

But the countryside in the southern Home Counties never really opens out. It is small country, carefully articulated and tended, everything in scale, no waste of the land and nothing to spare: its little hillocks rather like our own southern Berkshires, the roads and lanes careful interlineations in an orderly patchwork of pasture and plowland and neat villages. "No blustering summit or coarse gorge," the poet wrote of our own native Indiana:

> *... delirious nature*
> *Once in a lucid interval sobering here*
> *Left (repenting her extravagant plan)*
> *Conspicuous on our fields the shadow of man ...*

But that crap don't quite get it, as my commander used to say in Vietnam — for, tidy and tightly wrought as the land is in Surrey, I had the feeling it wouldn't have looked much different had nobody worked it or lived on it for the last hundred years. All was gray and brown and small; and quietly vital.

The train shot out of a tunnel and past a place called, so help me God, Dorking. Marjorie pulled at the lobe of my ear in time for me to see the sign on the platform and we began to laugh at it, and the children laughed too.

"Do you remember Maidenhead?" Marjorie asked. Of

9

course I did: I used to tear through Maidenhead in the old Healey when I lived in England. And wasn't there a place called Stule? Yes — and Shepherd's Bush? "You're foul," said Marjorie, and we laughed harder. Some of the passengers in the dining compartment looked up at us from their newspapers: Yes, yes, what is it, get on with it, and calmly went back to their reading. Then a man in brown worsted sitting across from us got up and walked to the end of the car and into the men's room and we were convulsed again. And once more, up from the newspapers came the heads, the eyes bovine but fully comprehending and unamused: The Americans think we're funny.

I looked away out the window at some English workmen riding black bikes along a road, noticing — it had been one of the first things that struck me when I was at Cambridge — that they still wore suit jackets instead of windbreakers or sweatshirts, and still wore those little hats that men in our country driving sports cars were wearing in the mid-50's. Suit jackets and Woodbine cigarettes strong enough to make dark spots on your lungs in a week's time, Ingo-land (as the song went) swinging with the perfect control of a pendulum, a land of dour efficiency and certitudes and biking along to work; the downing of tools and the workmen going home to their tellies and their pints of Mild in suburbs as bleak as Manayunk, P-A.

We were well past Dorking and clipping along through bare poplar groves under a smudgy dun sky, getting closer to Lawnsmere. Marjorie wondered where we'd come out if we didn't get off at Lawnsmere and I told her Portsmouth Harbor, explaining to her why the English 74's could never get the weather-gauge on the

French if they debouched into the Channel from Portsmouth, which was why the Royal Navy had preferred Plymouth, farther to the west.

"You pedant," she said, shaking her head. "And what were they going to do with the Grail when they found it, Mr. Rossetti?"

That got me thinking about the Stanley Cup and the NHL, and I also wondered if we could pick up the Giants' games off the European Armed Forces Network. The Giants, she said, good Lord. It didn't really matter to me in any case — the Giants were lousy that year — and the train was finally slowing down for Lawnsmere. And I was suddenly chastened by the thought that I was coming back to this country I had loved so well for so long, and that Lawnsmere was England in its very essence. The train could just conceivably have been the afternoon Congressional and Heathrow might have been Philadelphia International, God help us, but Lawnsmere was Lawnsmere. There was no other.

I got the children into their leashes for Marjorie and I asked them if they were excited. "I tooken my shobel from the plane," my son replied.

"Did you now, sir?" I opened the door of our compartment and pushed our suitcases out, and I put my arm around my wife and kissed her seriously for the first time in many weeks. My God, but we were happy.

At the same time, as we stepped onto the platform, I saw a man coming towards us and I asked Marjorie if this were Dorking. "No," she answered, "Shepherd's Bush." The man came closer, studying us.

"Mr. Adams, I think, the American? I have a car waiting for you outside."

We followed him into the parking lot wondering how

he recognized us so easily, and he got us all into the car and drove us along the High Street to the Rufus Arms, Lawnsmere.

2

We had come to England on an improbable business — my research for the biography of an English general long dead, a soldier familiar to readers of footnotes in Victorian histories as *Sandstone, Sir G., d. 1911.* The idea was that I should work in London, commuting daily from Lawnsmere. We had reservations at the Rufus Arms, a hotel of late Tudor origins named for a Norman king whose reputation must have had certain resonances with the attitudes and mores of late sixteenth century England.*

It won't hurt to tell you a few things about Lawnsmere before going any further with this narrative.

Namely: that the town was incorporated as a borough during the medieval period, and that it had, in 1970, a population of 7,120; that it is bisected by a torpid serpentine river some two hundred yards west of the High Street, called The Spley, a river now horribly polluted; and that it has: three hotels, of which the Rufus Arms is the most venerable, the least pretentious and most expensive; four public houses; a cobbled marketplace

---

*A contemporary chronicle says the following of this king, William II (Rufus), who ruled from 1087–1100. "Each night he went to bed a worse man than he had got up, and each morning he got up a worse man than he had gone to bed." He was fiery-faced, russet-haired, whoremongering, rambunctious and nasty and he was killed, perhaps accidentally, by an archer named Tyrrel.

dominated by a statue, strangely, of Clement Attlee; two chemists (drugstores) where you can buy English men's toiletries with names like "Centaur" and "Priapus" and john-paper with the consistency of fresh potato chips; no known whores; a jail and post office in the same building; a Jaeger's offering tweed jackets of such severe cut — I tried on several one day — that the circulation in your arms seems to be blocked; a boys' school, the grandest in all England, called St. Neot's; four squash courts; and several musty bookstores and antique shops.

The town has many other features, things too tedious to list at any length: semidetached red brick houses in long rows beyond the Spley; a smoggy, steeping climate most of the year; the famous Carnham Glass factory where the occupants of the red brick units work; and just beyond the ancient glacis of the town, gently undulating brown and putty-colored pasturage and thick copses of scrub pine and cedar. Lawnsmere is an orderly community: from the air I imagine it looks like one of those towns you build for an HO-gauged railway. About its history I learned more later.

In Lawnsmere, too, on Tuesday, December 18, 1971, lay one Frederick Giles, Jr., an American and a self-confessed Anglophile from the Midwest, a traveler resident in the Rufus Arms for the eleventh time in twenty-eight years. You will see, it is fair to say, that he had come to England partly to avoid the likes of us; and we — or I at any rate — partly to get away from people like him. This Giles was a fairly representative *mittelamerikan,* the kind of American you might expect to find in the Tower of London with a gleaming Pentax camera around his neck; or at home, hunkered down in front of the tube any Sunday afternoon in the fall.

Just like me, but with certain differences of value and style which will become apparent presently.

3

I first saw Giles in the pub of the Rufus Arms, an unprepossessing figure standing fifteen feet from Marjorie and me with his back towards us. "One of your countrymen," said Felix Carstairs, the innkeeper. In fact I had already discovered there was another American staying in the hotel, and that his name was Giles. The night porter's last duty before being relieved each morning was to lay out the day's mail on the counter of the cashier's nook in the lobby, and I had noticed an American airmail envelope in the pile as we checked into the Rufus Arms. This was its return address:

> *Mrs. F. Giles, Jr.*
> *Winnebago Terrace, Illinois*
> *U.S.A.*

I had nudged the letter for Marjorie to look at and asked her if she knew what a Winnebago was.

He had arranged himself at the bar in the classical attitude of the musing, solitary drinker: right foot mounted on the brass footrail, left foot back slightly for support, both elbows crooked on the bar. One hand I couldn't see; the other supported a slightly canted head, and there was a cigarette between its fingers — which, because of the placement of the hand, appeared to be sticking out of Mr. Giles's right ear.

He was dressed with some care in a well-fitted maroon velveteen smoking jacket, belted; trousers of distinctively English cut and heavy cavalry twill; diamond-patterned gray socks; crushed patent-leather moccasins. The edge of a wine-colored ascot necktie showed unevenly above the collar of Giles's jacket, and occasionally the hand holding the cigarette gave it a tug, as if it weren't staying up properly. The costume was right out of one of those "Young-Man-Wants-to-Make-$15,000-a-Year-Before-He's-Thirty" ads you used to see ten years ago.

Ignoring the current vogue, Giles had combed his hair back after the fashion of Mr. Robert Strange McNamara. Black, lank and shiny, it lay carefully plastered over an oblong bald spot just beneath the crown of his head. From time to time the head would incline to either side, attracted to the quiet murmur of conversation at both ends of the bar.

Despite his position, I could see Giles's posture was excellent, and that he kept himself in very good trim — a kind of squash player, NYAC trim accentuated by calf muscles that fairly bulged under the narrow trouser legs. This impression of cultivated athleticism was reinforced by a faintly rocking motion he kept up while he stood there, a continuous movement in which he seemed to be pushing against the bar, using his back foot as a kind of lever, pressing against the bar, and back again. It was like that Achilles-tendon stretch you see basketball players doing when they first come out on the floor.

In sum, when I think of my first impression of Giles, I remember a man of about five feet ten inches, well knit, vital and limber, and with the sartorial notions of a parvenu. But it is an impression too carefully reconstructed, I'm afraid, too much the product of what I saw and came to feel towards him later. Really, I hardly noticed him.

Meantime we had arranged to have dinner that night in the hotel restaurant with the owner Carstairs. He told us going in that he had asked Giles to join us; and so Giles did, twenty minutes later, walking confidently up to our booth at the quiet end of the dining room.

Mr. Giles, Mr. and Mrs. Adams. How d'ye do. How d'ye do. Mark? Yes, Mark. My wife Marjorie. Fred? No, not Fred, and not Freddie, either, if you don't mind, but Frederick. Frederick Giles. Well, how are you, sir? Real fine, yourself? Yes indeed, gray and penetrating, only 38° but it seems much colder. It *is* odd, it seems colder, it hits you when you get off at Heathrow, must be the Humboldt Current does it. The Humboldt Current? Whatever the hell it is — what's that current, Felix?

Ah, the Gulf Stream, good for you! Giles seemed in immense good humor, and he clapped Carstairs on the back and sat down next to Marjorie, across the table from me.

He had a striking face: feline from the mouth up, a face on first impression projecting a good deal of whimsy and perhaps — yes — guile. At the same time, below his mouth, it showed strength. The jaw was sharply protuberant and solid, and it was covered with a beard which — though shaved very close — shone almost blue in the candlelight.

The whole effect, however, was dominated by Giles's eyes. The pupils were hard and shiny — so hard, I remember thinking, that some sort of aching pressure must have been built up behind them, or that perhaps Giles was nearsighted and out of vanity would not wear his glasses publicly. The pupils stood out like tiny polished onyxes. The eyes arrested and fixed your attention in the same way a piercing shriek does, and Giles used them to great advantage, usually to fill up the vacuum of sentences he preferred not to finish, certain they could make his points for him. By themselves those eyes could express delight, rage, intense conviction, a kind of schoolmasterish disappointment with responses you might make to his infrequent questions, even pity; everything indeed except bathos and self-doubt: of which, it later became apparent, he had no sense.

Surprisingly Giles's hair was very thick in front, rising in a formidable widow's peak rooted in the sallow taut flesh of his forehead barely an inch above the cleavage between his eyebrows.

The face was extraordinarily mobile, a vehicle perfectly suited to express Giles's moods. When I say the lower jaw stuck out a bit, I don't mean to conjure up an image of some stolid artless bureaucrat; nor, when I say that if you were to see him only from the nose up, do I mean he might remind you of a small forest predator. As a matter of fact the impression you had was one of intelligence, an intelligence compounded of what the English call "cleverness" and what we call "moxie." Think of Ben Gazzara or John Cassavetes.

I suppose I should call him handsome. He was the kind of man other men always imagine attractive to women, even when they assure themselves they're better-looking. *Go talk to those girls, Giles — see if you can get them over to our table.* That kind of man. Someday he would be an old roué tooling around in a Toronado and a lime-green jacket, still fighting his age with Crunchy Granola and wheat germ and drinking-men's lunches and saunas, but he was not an old roué yet, not by a good ten years.

To all of which add the fact that his teeth were perfect, that he had a wide mouth with hard even lips, and that everything in his bearing bespoke a confidence in himself that verged on raw arrogance, and you have a very arresting animal indeed.

Giles cultivated certain idiosyncrasies of dress. Between the moment I saw him first in the public house and his arrival at dinner, he had changed from the smoking jacket ensemble to a navy blue suit. With it he wore some kind of silk shirt — but now here was something quite singular: he wore a necktie, but he had not, and he never did, run its thick end through the knot prepared to receive it. The tie therefore reminded you of a narrow bib; it was pulled quite straight from his Adam's apple to his waist, being held in place by an enameled American flag, a large one, excellently detailed. Once or twice at dinner I saw him give the necktie a tug and reset the patriotic tie clasp, and I noticed on his right pinkie a Mason's ring.

We had waited for Giles to order, but dinner came very quickly. He had called for the roast beef of old England, for everyone — causing Marjorie to shift a bit in her seat — but he had also announced the dinner was on him and that he knew the cuisine of the hotel like he knew the contours of his wife, and that its beef was "tender as a yam."

"A *yam*?" Carstairs asked, the way the English sometimes do when they know perfectly well the meaning of a word just used, but object to it on the grounds it is outside the ruck of common British usage.

"A yam, my friend, a bit of soul food." Giles winked

at me. "A staple et in the southern portion of our United States, consumed by the nether portion of our populace."

"You mean the blacks, then?"

"I do indeed."

"Ah."

Marjorie asked Giles what he was doing in Britain this time of year. Was it relaxation or business? Where was his wife?

He answered her deliberately, like an old judge instructing a jury. He had come to England in December to get away, or rather, to avoid the American tourists who ruined it in June and July. His visit, his eleventh stay in the hotel, was occasioned by the claims of both pleasure and business. He would be flying on to Glasgow, "in Scotland, north of here," in eight or ten days, to close a deal his firm had made with the Scots. As for Mrs. Giles, well, he saw as little of Dolores as he possibly could.

Were they divorced or separated, in that case?

Separated, but certainly not divorced. No woman was going to bilk him for alimony. In fact they enjoyed a perfect relationship: Giles sent her money enough to live comfortably, even to live in the style to which she wished to become accustomed. He paid the children's tuition bills at Culver and at Oberlin College. But he saw "the woman" only once or twice a year, and then only to address matters of detail. Very frankly, we wouldn't have liked her anyway. She did not behave well on trips: everything was such a big production for her. She could not, if we'd forgive his expression, un-ass herself like he could, just picking up her luggage and moving out, without making a terrible stink about it.

"You know what I mean, Adams?" he asked me.

I told him I certainly did. And prompted by the military cast of his language, I asked him if he'd ever been in the service.

"Quite a while back," he said, "several wars ago." He looked down at his salad and nodded ruefully. "I had my trigger time. But we can get into that later." Besides, neither the war nor the business about Dolores was important to him any more. The main thing was that he had come over because he loved England — not the grim and strike-ridden England of the modern period, the England of socialist parliamentarians and angry young men, but the England he used to know when he had visited here in the forties, during the war, the England that demonstrated everything that had made Carstairs' country great. "I've read literally hundreds of volumes of English history," he said.

Also — and he reckoned Carstairs would bear him out — the England we all loved and admired still lived on here in Lawnsmere, a town rich in traditions of both a military and literary character. He couldn't explain exactly why this was the case, nor would he bore us by trying, but time had not staled the infinite variety of the place, to quote the Bard, and thank God for that. Still a few places in the English-speaking world . . . and he patted Carstairs on the forearm.

The owner shrugged, perhaps still troubled by the yam. "Thank you, Frederick, but Lawnsmere's changing too."

"Well, yes, but not so much. Not so fast. People are civil to you here. Hell of a lot more civil to you than they are in Chicago, for instance. Where they're a damnsight more civil to you than they are in New York, Adams. We're not killing thirty people a week in Chicago. We got a strong mayor, not a pansy."

"I've heard Daley's a strong mayor."

"Tough as gristle" — and he piled the roast potatoes on his generous slices of overcooked beef, buried the whole under a glutinous gravy, and set to.

"Top off the old hopper," he said.

Later he asked Marjorie and me if we'd like to "recon the bar" with him. We did, but it was too crowded and too noisy to talk. An association football team was having a pre-Christmas party. "Looks like a goddam Brueghel painting," Giles said. "We'll do it tomorrow night."

We followed him upstairs and said our good nights in front of his door on the second floor.

"I got an oriel window in my room. You got one?"

"I don't think so." Actually, I hadn't noticed.

For a moment or two he lingered outside his door, like a man wondering if he'd said anything offensive. Finally he opened it, and with a raffish grin told me I had to admit Mayor Lindsay was a little bit spaced out.

"A little bit, like all of us." I shook hands with him and we walked down the corridor towards the staircase.

"See you in the morning," Marjorie called after him.

"Right. We'll have some fun here."

"See you, Fred."

"Frederick," I heard, and the door closed behind him.

4

It was still dark when I started waking up. Far away I heard the gentle clattering, the muffled retreat, of a train.

It must have reminded me of a troop-train hurtling south from Wilmington, on into the night, deeper and deeper into the American South with its sweated cargo of fitful sleepers, exhausted soldiers, leaving behind them their Boston and New York and Philadelphia, going down to training depots to prepare for the Pacific wars; soldiers torn brutally from their families like legs torn from insects by vicious children. On their lips remained the waxy tastes of the young women they had kissed in the stations. The women had worn swishing, short-hemmed, white dresses with shoulder pads in them, and they had chewed gum and cleaned their nails with bobby pins, and the soldiers were remembering these things, and smoking, and playing cards and going off to danger, perhaps to die. They were not naval officers like my father, not of that Princetonish, Proust-reading ilk, the young freemasonry of lawyers and businessmen who would reappear in the fifties mowing lawns on Sundays in faded khakis. The drill sergeants were going to meet these soldiers' trains in the wan hours of another day and shave their heads and teach them to kill and muscle them around; and then they would die in the volcanic ash and coral of the islands we had to capture.

But my father would die, *did* die with them, "Jackie" Adams whom everyone loved died with them, and I was groping desperately for my mother. We were going to be alone together always, and I thought I heard her smile gently in the dark, listening to the train fading in the warm night. *Miss Phoebe Snow, about to go, along the road, to Buff-alo. Her gown stays white, from morn to night, upon the road, of anthracite.*

It was warm and fragrant in the room, and my mother touched the hair on my forehead with the tips of her fingers. He'll be alright, darling, of course he'll be alright. But he was not. I turned my head from her, awakening, flailing, aware of the soft contact of my pillow with the wall across the room, drawing and pulling myself out of the terror that held me like an impossibly soft but relentlessly constricting vise. The memories tumbled about me, faded like the sun behind a thunderhead, leaving me sweating and exhausted, my body hot against Marjorie's.

"Darling?"

I sat upright and my feet went to the cold polished floor and I remembered I was in Lawnsmere, in England. I looked out the open window of our bedroom and stared at the ochre balloons of haze masking the streetlamps of the High Street, a prospect as bleak as the formless residue of my dream.

I came sharply awake and tried to throw over the memory.

The Rufus Arms Hotel overlooks the High, and the *Egdon Rooney Guide* I had been reading before going to sleep was not silent on this situation. Its querulous pomposities about the hotels and inns of Great Britain included the rich snot of the following, referring to the hotel: "an hotel set on a highway can be the source of much unpleasantness to those in residence therein."

In fact, I must say, after I clear my throat, I must say that I never found the situation unpleasant, and that I came to look forward to waking up in our creaking oblong bedroom and hearing the sounds that carried to it from the street. At intervals of five or six minutes one heard the shrill keening of tires, followed by silence, succeeded suddenly by a great sizzling whoosh which would send small shudders through the hotel — at this hour lorries shouldering up from the south coast, muscling their way up to London: trucks packed with machines and tools and staple grains, heavy trailers full of tiny European cars — the world makes, England takes — their drivers freshly battened at the transport café just below Lawnsmere, barely beyond the rim of sound; trucks hurrying on to London before the traffic began building and clogging, going north to clot the ring roads and sustain the city.

I went to the window and looked down at the street, almost expecting to see a bobby in a felt pickelhaube ambling along with his nightstick. But I looked down to nothing. Not a paper scudded on sidewalk or gutter. The High was empty of people and sound, empty absolutely of motion, of life, of the barest vestige of whatever holiday celebrating there had been the evening before. I leaned over the windowsill on my palms, remembering too late how disgusting Marjorie thought it was that I was too lazy to clear my phlegm in the bathroom. I heard the mattress give with her awakening and at the same time let fly a fine hawking lunger at the nearest street-lamp.

"Who do you think you are, Jack Kennedy?"

We have the famous picture of the musing young president in our study in New York, the last thing I see each night before I go into our bedroom.

But Marjorie had not heard me spit, had only woken up and seen my silhouette at the window.

"Who do you think *you* are? Mandy Rice-Davies? Christine Keeler?" I felt her hand go around my waist, and it pulled me backward towards her on the bed. I leaned around, over her, and kissed her. "You do love me,

Mark, don't you?" she asked, and I answered her, "Sure, Christine, I love you."

She lay back flat and brought her hands together on her chest.

"You're never serious any more," she said, as from a distance, as though she were talking in her sleep.

I told her I was more serious then than I had ever been, that she was more precious to me at that moment than she had been the day we were married.

"I used to love waking up with you in Connecticut when it snowed," she murmured.

" 'When hushed awakenings are dear.' "

"Don't quote things all the time."

I got up from the bed again, a bit wounded by her remark.

"Don't be mean," she said. "The minute you get vertical, you get mean."

"Darling, I'm not even awake."

"I don't turn you on."

"Of course you turn me on."

But already Marjorie had turned away towards the far wall, gathering up her legs fetally. "You run off to your little research," she said. "I'm going back to sleep. Don't wake your children."

I have always been suspicious of people who seem certain about almost anything. Looking back at our stay in Lawnsmere I can see that on this account alone I was bound to feel some sort of prejudice against Frederick Giles. I thought of him as I dressed that morning, and I remembered Marjorie's telling me she had arranged to have lunch with him while I was in London. This was fine, of course. I wanted her to have fun while I was working.

But if I am prejudiced against people who project the cocksureness, the confidence of utterance, which had been almost the first thing I had noticed about Giles and which even now I best remember about him, still I admire men whose airs of determination and certitude seem to mask lurking and troubling memories and obligations, men who can put away their pains and their doubts so the world can only guess at their presence and can never judge their dimensions. I think, for example, of the roles Clifton Webb used to play in the movies of twenty or thirty years ago. I remember Webb as perpetually bounding from his bed, standing close-lipped in icy showers, whistling while he made his ablutions, dressing and breakfasting and flicking his walkingstick from a rack in the shining fresh hallway, striding confidently down an empty morning street. The dim clinging remembrance of dreams like the one I had had, the recollection, perhaps, of unhappy lovemaking, his private joyless concerns: these he could seem to have abandoned as effortlessly and quietly as a motorboat burbles away from a pier.

I can never do this. My dreams are almost always dreams in which I grope and reach out for receding, fading treasures and assurances: for love, once for my father, then for my mother only, finally sometimes for Marjorie. But I cannot hold these things in my dreams, cannot grasp them, and I wake up longing and empty.

It had been years since I had thought or dreamed about my father and his terrible death in the war. Perhaps it was some phrase of Giles's at dinner — "trigger time," "several wars ago," or whatever — that had made me dream my dream. In any case I remember that my mood of sadness and despair that morning was dissipated only on the train up to London, and only then because I was thinking about Giles, wondering why he had come to Lawnsmere; wondering, even, what his being in the Rufus Arms might mean to our own visit.

5

The National Army Museum in Chelsea, where Sir Gordon Sandstone's papers are kept, does not open till ten. The place is run mainly by Chelsea pensioners, retired soldiers who look after its exhibits and in their mild ingratiating way provide its "security." I imagine the ten o'clock opening time was established out of consideration for these old warriors, for they are often very old men, and many of them have been wounded in England's wars.

The Lawnsmere train got to Waterloo just after eight, so I decided to walk from the station to Chelsea, a distance — if you keep close to the Thames when you can — of just over four miles.

I loved London better than any city in the world, and it had been almost seven years since my last, and valedictory, visit. I walked that chilly morning over Waterloo Bridge and then west along the Embankment on the north side of the Thames, past relics and trophies and statues of great men, testimonials to an age so certain of its power and stature that it often commemorated even its lesser heroes by their surnames only, without epitaph or explanation, on the marble plinths below the statues. To Americans the men thus honored are obscure. It is as though you had come upon the statute say, of William Harrison's vice-president or the inventor of hexachlorophene in Central Park: MORTON. JONES. Who were they? But the Victorians knew the significance of what their heroes had wrought, or thought they did; and they were so certain that generations unborn must celebrate these lives and deeds as they did that they felt no need to explain them — or, by implication, to explain themselves. The names come at you with the effect of cold magisterial inscrutability: GORDON. ABERCROMBY. SPEKE. Or whoever.

Marjorie is bored by such things. We cannot share them. She would have called the statues mawkish, or "too much." And indeed, as I strode along the river, I was conscious that much of my happiness in coming back to London had something to do with the fact that she and the children weren't with me. She would have been bored by Whitehall too, and by the Life-guardsman keeping their watch outside the Old War Office Building, and by Westminster Hall and the grand statues of Cromwell and Richard outside Parliament; she would have been bored and the children impatient.

Yet abruptly I was disgusted myself, if not bored, by what certain sections of London seemed to have become since I had seen them last: by the very ambience that would have stimulated and pleased Marjorie. By Chelsea, for instance, Chelsea with its King's Road shops which displayed faded combat fatigues guaranteed to have been worn by American soldiers in Indochina and advertised at "Two Gns"; Chelsea with the skittish, sham unctuousness of its Pakistani waiters, now lolling in doorways of restaurants and coffeebars; with its shabby reproductions of American institutions: bare, sleek little supermarkets and tinselly chemists, boutiques, pet stores with kinkajous and ocelot kittens in their windows; newspaper kiosks full of smudgy flapping pornographic posters . . .

And everywhere lank-hipped, lank-haired girls: tight-breasted, lissome, arch; girls clustering around the windows of the smart shops, girls moving along sinuously in pairs — beautifully matched pairs, too, not the usual Grace Kelly plus a pig combinations I remembered from my own adolescence, the ugly one perpetually suspicious, always trying to get the good-looking one to go to the bathroom with her. No, these girls were all beautiful. They all seemed to be talking about their beaux: David or Jeremy or Adrian. Silly young men, I imagined them, mousy progeny of Tory commerce who would take them to places with names like The Garrison or The Fanta . . .

I wondered what Giles would have made of them. To me they looked elusive and haughty, lacking in substance, bored. For a moment I envisioned a faceless full-bodied Englishwoman slithering out of a diaphanous minislip, cool and amused while I fumbled with a zipper. ("He's funny, that Napoleon," said Josephine to her friends in Paris, showing them his desperate love letters . . .) Giles, I decided, would be the type that favored therapeutic ravishings of women like this. He would teach them a lesson; whereupon they would respond gloriously and would cease babbling about their Adrians and Jeremys.

I remembered the expression on his face when Marjorie asked about his own estranged wife, how coldly deliberate his answer had been. *No woman is going to bilk me for alimony*. It would have been entertaining to have his comments on these birds of Chelsea.

An hour later in the Army Museum a pensioner brought me the Sandstone Papers. I asked him if the Museum's library had anything on county or borough history. I didn't feel like attacking the Papers that morning but I was curious about Lawnsmere and its attraction for Giles. He had read hundreds of books about English history and been here many times. What kept luring him back to Lawnsmere and the Rufus Arms?

"Something a tourist might want, sir?"

I told the pensioner this would be fine, anything for a tourist that treated the counties of England separately.

"Which county had you in mind, sir?"

I told him Surrey, and he padded down the hall like an old footman. In five minutes he had returned and *The Tourist's Guide to England Past and Present* lay open before me. The entry for Lawnsmere, Surrey, signed at the end with the initials and date *J. McC. A. F., 1954*, is, in its ornate whimsicality and its preoccupation with the frivolous detail the writer must have expected the tourist would want, worth quoting in part:

> Lawnsmere as it appears today was laid out in the late six-teenth century, between the year of the Armada and the accession of the first Stuart king, James. In that time there appears to have been a concerted attempt to clear away what the labours of several centuries had established over the ancient town centre — jerry-built houses and the like — and an effort, too, to straighten the streets and make them intersect at useful places. Indeed the superimposed sixteenth century grid lends an unexpected tone to the town, an inflexion of orderliness and clear-headed purpose. Streets do not ramble in Lawnsmere.

The history of the town is ancient and distinguished. In the time of the first Richard it was a flourishing centre for overland trade in rude cloths; and long before that, its cast had always been rather military. Whether, in the pre-Christian era, Matthew Arnold's dark Iberians and shy traffickers had ventured this far inland is unknown; but there is a tradition that a tiny reconnaissance party from the second Caesarian expedition (54 B.C.) came to the site of the present town. Certain military implements attributed to this date were found in Lawnsmere in 1936, and with them some ancient Roman coins. Suddenly the town seduced the country's attention; but it basked in the light of its fame for three days only, being displaced in the papers by the news of Edward VIII's intention to marry Mrs. Simpson. Lawnsmere remained only the focus of a long and earnest scholarly debate, *viz*: had the coins and weapons been secreted there some two thousand years *after* the time of Caesar? — by crafty townsmen anxious to establish Lawnsmere's antiquity and therefore willing to provide the "evidence" for it? Or, as Professor ffolke-Cantlay has argued in the *Journal for Historical Research Studies* (vol. LXII, pp. 465–477) were these evidences genuine, the natural detritus of any small expedition, objects lost or discarded by a careless soldiery? Like all such arid controversies, this one generated more heat than light; it continued to be prosecuted with *brio* on both sides. As recently as 1953, an American who had driven down from Guildford claimed to have found more of the coins, but these were pronounced fradulent by the authorities: they bore the inscription LV, B.C.! But the American had gulled a reporter or two. The public controversy resumed briefly, ran again along more serious and subterranean channels, and finally was forgotten . . .

The Roman Empire seemed to erode inwardly; the centre did not hold: the torso fell away, became flaccid, incriminating the extremities in its own dissolution. The process lasted several centuries. Soldiers were withdrawn from the local garrison (as they were pulled back from garrisons all over Britain) to put down certain revolts across the Channel in Gaul, the European commanders promising to return the troops as soon as they had dealt with the rebels. But the soldiers did not return, and by degrees their numbers and influence shrank until, by the sixth century, they had gone completely, vanishing almost without a trace. The fort decayed; small boys mocked its former strength with axes and fire arrows; and the invading Jutes would have little patience with such lingering reminders of the race that had preceded them and oppressed the populace they now undertook to rule. . . .

In the fifteenth century Lawnsmerians of stature inclined to the Yorkist cause, offering sanctuary on two occasions to the leading followers of Richard of York, and later to his son Edward. The latter, who reigned as Edward IV, is mentioned in a contemporary account as having "laine here at Lawnsmere with the Mistresse Shore full three nighte" in the year 1471; probably, one imagines, to the proper-active and officious clucking of the local housewifery and the *schadenfreude* of their husbands. The "Shore Bed" — in which their lust for each other was at least three times assuaged — is still to be seen, incidentally, in the house of the present owner of the Rufus Arms hotel, already mentioned . . .

We pass over the Glorious Revolution the town would just as soon forget and its demure pleasure at the news of the death of William III. By now it had grown to a shape and size which would have made it recognizable to one of its modern citizens. Its population (round about 7,000) has fluctuated no more than four percent between 1742 and 1951. Then, as now, Lawnsmere's was a service economy, and then, as today, it was the county seat of many who had made money in ways the aristocracy of the land affected to despise. And in 1742, by coincidence, was founded midway between Liphook and Lawnsmere one of the great English public schools, St. Neot's, more truly the nursery of English statesmanship than any other foundation, and at the present day comprising 850 boys and 96 masters. The road from St. Neot's to Christ Church, Oxford, to the House of Commons, to the Cabinet has been as broad and durable as the aforementioned Roman roads in Surrey . . .

Several incidents took place in the town during the nineteenth century to which Lawnsmerians point with some pride. Lord Nelson stopped in the town's largest hotel, the Rufus Arms, on his way south to his flagship *Victory*, death, and everlasting glory. In the public room of the hotel he relived the battle of Aboukir for a gathering of transfixed hail-fellows by moving saltcellars around his tabletop, whilst (according to local legend) a bumptious young barmaid sat on his knee knowing very well that if she fell backward no arm would catch her. Two future prime ministers were among those in the audience — schoolboys then, on French leave from St. Neot's: and their essays in international diplomacy and their proclivities for participation in the making of tactical plans as well as grand strategy later became notorious in the Foreign Office and the Admiralty. Tourists still sit at the famous old table drinking the admiral's health.

The same hotel served also as a refuge for those who found the world too much with them: three eminent Victorians among these. Tennyson stayed here during the early months of his bereavement following the death of Hallam. He is remembered as having sat at the Nelson table for hours at a time smoking acrid shag tobacco and drinking Cerise Madeira in an unavailing effort to exorcise his terrible grief. "Poor b_____, he never learned how to swim," he is supposed to have kept saying, though this is manifest nonsense, since Hallam did not die a swimmer's death.

Nor should the tourist credit the tale that George Eliot and Henry Lewes used the Rufus Arms as a trysting place, or that they demanded the use of the Shore Bed, then the property of another Lawnsmere Inn, The Frightened Cardinal. The visitor who sees the bed will realize in an instant that this venerable berth couldn't have held either of these distinguished *littérateurs*.

Indeed stories like these are bound to be discovered in any English town, and the present writer is inclined to think their veracity is less important than their probability; or even than the *possibility* that the events they describe really happened. Tennyson's comment on life after death strikes him as entirely relevant: "the likelihood of eternal life is sufficient for men to believe in if they find it comforting . . ."

The article ran on in this vein for another two or three pages. I will spare you my reflections on how very

"English" were its style and cavalier treatment of the facts. Besides, I already had enough information about Lawnsmere to understand its appeal for a gentleman from Winnebago Terrace.

It was early afternoon. After lunch I went back to the station by cab and caught a train for Lawnsmere. One thing I might mention: about a half mile out — the train was moving very slowly through a railyard and rocking like an old trolley — we passed a train on the next track going the other way. In one of its first-class compartments sat an English gentleman wearing black-rimmed Charlie Chan glasses and looking out the window over his copy of the *Times*. For a microsecond our eyes engaged. He gave me such a look of hauteur as I have never seen before or since, a look which seemed to me to sum up everything I had been reading about in the piece on Lawnsmere, a fixed snotty stare which affirmed both the vanished supremacy of England and the Englishman's belief in the irrelevance of its passing.

I have no idea why I did it, but I gave him the finger.

6

Marjorie was lying on a faded chintz chaise in the sitting room when I got in. She was wearing a housecoat I have always disliked, a rag that dated from our days at Fort Hall, cinched at the neck like a carcanet by a ribbon. She heard me come in but did not move, keeping on with an idle flipping of pages through the British magazine *Queen*. The room was a depressing shambles of toys and suitcases overflowing with cosmetic bottles and neckties, and the prospect, after my day in London, put me in a foul mood. From the adjoining room the children shrieked. The sitting room smelled vaguely fecal. Suddenly an egg-salad sandwich hurtled through the air and splattered down the front of my shirt: "Daddy!" I went directly into the bathroom.

"A loving greeting," Marjorie said.

"I'll be right out." I had been reading on the train about plaque, a kind of mold that formed on your teeth. I scrubbed away at it.

"How'd it go, darling?"

"Alright. I'll be right out."

"I had a sandwich with Mr. Giles in the pub at lunch."

"Where were the children?"

"They were there, climbing around, being obnoxious."

"What'd they make of Mr. Giles?"

"He was awfully nice to them. Very patient with them."

"Look," I said, "if you don't like the way I deal with my children come on out and say it."

"Deal with. What do you think they are, cattle? Soldiers?"

"What'd you talk about at lunch?"

"Lot of things. Art."

"Art? He know anything?"

"I think he may know a lot. He said his favorite painter was Parmigianino."

"Parmigianino, my ass. Looks like life is one bullshit-artist after another, doesn't it?"

"He seemed to know what he was talking about. He said we had a lot in common with the Mannerists."

"What's that supposed to mean?"

"He thinks people from New York are pretentious."

"He comes on strong, doesn't he?" I threaded my way through the road graders, dolls, and dump trucks on the floor and put out my wrists to have Marjorie fix my cuff links. "Doesn't know us from Shinola and he's saying people from New York are pretentious. That's a bit much, isn't it?"

"One day in London and you're saying 'a bit much.' That's probably what he means."

"Parmigianino any good?"

Marjorie doesn't like the way I formulate questions about art. When I'm in a bad mood I make it a point to ask if such-and-such a painter is "any good." Like, is Stottlemyre any good?

"Rather precious, I should have thought."

"You should have thought. I know his type. Their favorite painter's Norman Rockwell and they say it's Fragonard. They name somebody no one ever heard of and think they're one up on you."

"You should talk, fella."

"Who else was there? Was Mr. Carstairs there? I liked him."

Mr. Carstairs was there. So was his daughter Deirdre. A whole collection of people from Lawnsmere. In the absence of her Uncle Orme Goderich, the Western Desert colonel, who was away until Friday, they would have to be Marjorie's entertainment.

She fixed a cuff link and lifted my wrists to her shoulders and put up her face to be kissed, "not on the forehead, either," she said, and I kissed her hard on the lips, remembering the girls I had seen on King's Road, and my mother's old reassurance that married love was different, and better. At this point, interrupting a scene that seemed to give her much pleasure and some little embarrassment, Mrs. Nance, the hotel sitter, walked into the room. I made small talk with her until Marjorie was ready, and we went down to the pub to keep our date with Giles.

7

He was standing alone at the bar, and when he heard us come in he spun around to greet us and told us to grab the Nelson Table. "Right here," he said, pointing at it. "You want a highball, don't you, same as last night?"

"Thank you," I said, "a highball would be dandy." We sat down and waited for our highballs.

It was a warm and, for England, even sensuous room we sat in. Its paneling was dark and mottled, and the owner had had the good sense not to cover it with *Vanity Fair* cartoons or pictures of the rowing VIII from St. Neot's. Only a single picture had been hung, this between the two windows looking out on the High, a nondescript painting of an Indian dhow canting before a storm, and bearing the legend "Boat on the Carnatic Coast." The open floor area, about the size of your living room, was covered with a worn Herez rug whose original orderly tangle of colors now merged in a kind of lugubrious dark purple. The rug was worn thin in paths which radiated out from the center of the bar to the tables like thick brown spokes, and an enormous blackened fireplace in perpetual use kept the room warm and stimulated a sense of good fellowship and easy tolerance. This was a room in which you could imagine athletes foregathering to drink off an unexpected defeat.

As for the bar, its equipage was paleolithic. Each drink received a single forlorn ice cube spooned out of a tin basket. Little crackers in the shape of fish were set out on the bar for hors d'oeuvres, but the wicker serving-baskets which held them were never refilled. You got one ounce precisely of seventy-two proof whiskey for your twenty-five new pence, so drunks did not come cheaply or quickly. The barstools were unsafe to sit upon.

"You be pleasant to him," Marjorie whispered with an odd urgency. "That's what they call drinks in the Midwest."

"Certainly I'll be pleasant to him. I've just had a rough day, that's all. I'm beat."

Giles moved towards us in a kind of sashay, concentrating on not spilling the drinks. He sat down next to Marjorie, facing me across the square tabletop.

"Have a good day?"

"Not bad," I told him. "Yourself?"

"A very good day. Considerably enlivened, if I may say so, by a delightful luncheon with your frau."

"And my kinder, too, I understand."

"Touché. Sprechen sie deutsch?"

"Prost." I raised my glass to him, thinking we were really in for it tonight. We had come all the way to Surrey to have a highball with Winnebago Terrace, Ill., with an American flag on his tieclasp. Meantime he was drinking off his whiskey in one heavy swallow.

"Hell," he said, "I can't remember enough kraut to order a bockwurst. But as a matter of fact, what German I do know I learned in a POW Camp in '44–'45, in War Two."

In War Two. "What were you, in the Air Force?"

"Yes, sir. I was in the Twenty-Fourth Tactical Bomb Wing. We flew out of Rostarn Field, about ten miles from here. That's when I got to know Lawnsmere and the hotel and this table, where Lord Nelson once sat. It was a veritable island of serenity in a warriors' world."

"Ball-turret gunner?"

"That's it, they washed me out with a hose. No, I had a commission. I was copilot on a B-24. First lieutenant."

"Cut any ice in prison camp, being a lieutenant?"

"Sure as hell didn't."

"How'd the krauts treat you?"

"The Germans?" He looked at me sternly. "Our allies, now. They treated me pretty good, pretty well."

"Try to escape?"

"We were firming up plans when we got liberated. You know, Adams, people have this half-assed notion outta *Hogan's Heroes* or somewhere that prison camp was like a prep school — horsing around, people playing catch, people digging underground with spoons and taking the soil out of the barracks one pocketful at a time. It wasn't like that at all. You couldn't tunnel most of the time because the ground was frozen in the first place. We were going to force an egress underground in the early summer of '45, and we might have made it if we'd gone through with it. But by then the war was over, and it woulda been over a lot sooner if that son-of-a-bitch Eisenhower had done what he should have."

"What was that?"

"Gone right to Berlin, got there ahead of Zoo-kawv. We could have done it no sweat. The Russians were raping everything in sight, they weren't pressing. Eisenhower and Roosevelt coulda gone right through."

"But they sold us down the river at Potsdam?"

"Not down the river. Up the creek. You guessed her."

Marjorie's uncle had tried to escape three times and I wondered briefly whether she would bring him into the conversation: the elegant Orme Goderich, who would no more talk about his exploits in the war, or make excuses for his failures to escape, than he would have volunteered information about his own unhappy marriage. Even at that point it crossed my mind that Giles and Goderich would be an interesting match. But Marjorie thought I was putting Giles on. She asked him what he thought about Vietnam.

"What *about* Vietnam, honey?"

"We could have gone right through there too?"

"Hell, yes. We coulda gone in there loaded for bear and cleaned it up in a month, or less."

"Bombed them into the Stone Age?"

"Hey, Susan" — he called for the barmaid — "bring this here uptight liberal another drink." And to Marjorie, pointing at me: "Whose your cousin, here? He's a menace! . . . Bring me a double," he added.

He was in excellent humor. "Lemme lay an old LBJ on ya, boy." So saying, he reached out and grabbed one of my elbows in his hand. "Let us reason tigither on this matter. You stay good and calm, Adams, and I'll give you my theory."

Now he had thought about the matter very seriously and for a hell of a long time, just like me. OK? The issue was a *hell* of a lot simpler than people made it out to be in the *New York Times*. Now, mind you, he held no brief for cobalt belts or doomsday machines or any of that Dr. Strangelove BS. *But:* "It is the sal-ient characteristic of the liberal *arriviste* who does not study war seriously or study people like the English thinker Burke that he makes those on the Right out to be wild men. Don't deny it, Adams."

Getting back to Vietnam: Hell, we didn't *need* that kind of overkill on people like the Viet Minh or their "successors by default," the Viet Cong. No. What had been indicated at an early stage was an Inchon-type operation, very surgical and efficient, in which the United States deployed ten or twelve divisions right off the bat. Four for the South, say, but up along the DMZ, to fix the enemy's attention and get his troops moving in that direction, the other six to land at a major coastal city "like Hanoi," there to bring almighty smoke on the North, disrupt their communications with their armies in the South and convince the little bastards they were playing Triple-A Ball with a Big League team. The key was lightning-quick speed.

Now what all this was was a simple way of saying to your enemy that he must cease and desist or — for the first time we saw what we would learn to recognize as Giles's most characteristic gesture — "splat!" His right hand shot up in a fist, hung poised for a second until we both looked at it, then dropped, wrist onto waiting palm, into his left.

About halfway through his explanation Giles had become serious. The friendly banter had given way to a kind of military briefing. Now, just as abruptly, he recovered himself. Briefly he massaged his temples, his brow creasing in unconvincing remorse and heavy concentration, communicating the pain it gave him to talk so tough. War was awful, but long wars were worse than short ones.

"Let's get to the theory of it and be more dispassionate, OK?"

I told him to fire when ready.

"The Germans had a military philosopher called Clausewitz — you both know who he was — and he said that war is an expansion of political intercourse by different means. You with me?"

"We're with you," Marjorie said.

"OK. Now with all due respect to the little lady, here, that's bullshit. It's one of the ironies of history that one of the great warrior-races produced a philosopher who made such a lousy assessment of how wars were fought, and how they should be fought. Don't kid yourself: war's not the expansion of politics. Where politics ends, *that's* where war takes over. You give that general a hunting license and you turn his ass loose."

"Serious?"

"Hell, yes, I'm serious."

"Well," I said, "but within reasonable limits, right?"

"If the general's any good he'll stay within reasonable limits. If he's not, he shouldn't be a general."

Giles never gave you much time to digest his *pronunciamentos,* and I'm not a quick thinker. I remember that at the time I really didn't feel like talking seriously about war or Vietnam, and thinking that his reasoning was bizarre. Yet he was so ardent, so concerned that we understand his point of view, so solicitous of Marjorie's sensibilities — the swearing notwithstanding — that I decided not to change the subject. He went on.

"OK. You tell that general, whoever he is, you tell him to go in and win the war. Here's *x*-thousand troops. You win the war, I'll worry about politics."

"What would you have done with MacArthur in Korea?"

Giles leaned forward as though he didn't want anyone but Marjorie and me to hear his answer. "Listen," he said, "you got two people competing to fight the war. Am I right? OK. You got the greatest strategist of the twentieth century and you got a pale little haberdasher in granny glasses. Which one you gonna take? Talk about Vietnam, crow, there wouldn't be any Vietnam now if we'd listened to MacArthur. Yalu River, my ass."

Marjorie dangled her fingers in her highball, absently stirring its vanishing ice cube. Though she was not looking at Giles I was sure she must have the same heavy sense of *déjà vu* that I had; we had heard the arguments before: the relentlessly confident enunciations of a conviction so simple, so guileless, that its spokesmen could hardly believe men disagreed with them about it. As mesmerizing and predictable as it was exasperating, it seemed cast in a kind of sonata form: statement, embroidery, summation. Indeed, I must admit a certain sense of envy for people like Giles, men for whom things seemed so simple — though I certainly wasn't aware of it while Giles was talking. I remember Marjorie saying in the '68 campaign, "Mr. Agnew goes right to sleep at ten. He's sure, and you're not." What I was thinking at that point was that Giles was using his OK's like a jack lifting a car: each OK was a pawl; higher and higher up the ratchet he jacked you, imagining you were buying all the premises.

But what the hell? He was entertaining, and the liquor and fatigue made him easy to listen to. I kept at him: "If MacArthur had bombed China, Russia would have attacked Berlin. We had no troops to speak of in Europe then, did we?"

"Didn't need 'em, Adams. We had the You-Know-What. We coulda told Mos-cao, look, any monkey business outta you . . ." Again the "splat" gesture.

Marjorie excused herself to go to the ladies' room and Giles abandoned his diatribe to watch her walk away from us, his eyes riveted on what he later called her "callipygian amplitudes." I even thought I saw him swallow.

"That's one of the things you look for in a woman, Adams, that outflare kinda business where their waist goes out and down. A good paira hips and you could put marbles on either side and they wouldn't roll off. Pretty classy young lady, right there."

"Thank you, sir."

"No, she is — really a sweet girl."

"Tolerant, too."

"Yeah, she must hear a lot of talks like this — where was I? Oh yeah, and you're gonna ask me whether or not I'd unleash Chiang too, right?"

"Would you have?"

"You're fucking-ay!" he affirmed joyously. With Marjorie gone and the barmaid out of the room he could say what he damn well pleased. I thought of a movie I'd seen in which the Bomb was shown nestled in its bay just before the switch had been pulled to drop it. On its nose was the salutation "Hi there."

"Adams," Giles said, "let me tell you something, alright?"

"Please."

"We're gonna hit it off real good. I like a man like yourself, well-set-up young man, got his shit together, thinks about important issues. All you have to do is don't get hot under the collar, right?"

I nodded. At that moment I wanted very much to be agreeable.

Marjorie now returned, followed through the doors by a couple I had not seen in the hotel before, a middle-aged man with a beefy pink face and a lissome ash-blonde at least twenty years his junior. "Gangbusters," I said, watching her.

"Bad face, Adams, bad face. How many times you followed a beautiful bod down the platform of a station and found it belonged to a pig?"

"All the time."

He brooded. "It *does* happen all the time. You stand in line in front of your Maker and he gives one guy an IQ of one fifty and a face like Socrates. Or they give a woman like her a bod like that and she comes on with a face like Native Dancer."

Suddenly he seemed rheumy and depressed. I began wondering how long he had been drinking before Marjorie and I came down. As a matter of fact, the woman at the bar was a real stunner, face included, so glamorous and self-possessed I wondered who she was, whether Giles had perhaps once made a blundering pass at her and found he disgusted her. Or if he made crude remarks about anyone beautiful but out of his range.

"She's untouchable, Adams," I heard him whisper. "Regular Joan Fontaine type, string-a-pearls, cashmere suit. You know that type if you're from New York. You see them watching plays. The lummox who brought her in's her uncle. Besides" — he stopped whispering — "married to someone like this it shouldn't make any difference to you, should it?" And he actually ran the backs of his fingers down the length of Marjorie's arm and winked at her. "Should it?"

"You're right, it doesn't."

"But you can read the menu even if you can't order — right?"

"My better half has reservations about that, too."

"Yeah? Jealous female, huh?" He looked carefully at her. "Where'd you meet this young stud?" he asked her. "No. Wait, lemme guess. Allow me to *ex-trapo-late* from your appearance etcetera where you met and who you are."

"You mean where we're at," she said.

I loathed this sort of thing. The Hitler tabletalk was diverting, tolerable: Giles was an authentic original. His language, a pastiche of cliché and inkhorn words and spleen, focused your attentions on himself, not on the banalities he was uttering. Now, perhaps, he felt that we had had enough of that; he would try to ingratiate himself with us — or was it some crude *politesse?* — by getting us to talk about ourselves. Where we met and who we were.

"Let's see, Adams, I figure you for an Ivy League product. Not Harvard — too solid for that, maybe Brown. Isn't there a college calls itself Brown? I used to know a guy in the Air Force who went to Dartmouth. Used to sing 'What's the color of horseshit? Brown, Brown, Brown.' My dear woman, I *do* apologize. But there is such a place, no? And you, Mistress Quickly, Smith for you, ay? The both of you met on the tailgate of a ranchwagon at a football game. They play lousy football in the Ivy League so you ignored it and fell in love. How's that?"

"Very perceptive, Mr. Giles," Marjorie answered. "I didn't go to Smith. Mark didn't go to Brown. And I never sit down on tailgates."

"That's what tailgates are for, honey, tail."

"That'll, do, Fred-baby," I said.

"OK. No pique — right? You didn't go to Brown, so where'd you go?"

"He went to Princeton, Mr. Giles. I spent the first ten years of my life in England. Then I went to school in America, and then to college in Wellesley, Mass."

"Where's that?"

"Near Boston." Marjorie's voice had a real edge on it. "Be pleasant, dear," I said to her.

"I heard of Wellesley. Place with a lotta class, right?"

"Quite right, Mr. Giles, lots and lots of class. Racket clubs. A chaise longue in every room and a Bergdorf tuck-shop in the basement of the gym."

"You know what I mean."

"We know what you mean."

"Why'd you leave England? Your parents limey?"

"No, Father's American, Mother's part English."

"What were they doing in England?"

"He was a diplomat and he married my mother here."

"Ah. He for God only, she for God in him."

"What do you mean by that?"

"Forget it. What was he doing in England?"

"I told you, a diplomat."

"Ambassador?"

"No, minister."

"So a career civil servant, then. They never give St. James to a professional. As a matter of fact, that's why Anglo-American relations have been so rotten since '45.

They stick in some creep of a liberal newspaperman and he grosses out the British. So you came back when he got reassigned."

"Came back when he got reassigned."

"Where'd you go then?"

"New York. He works in Wall Street and we lived in New Jersey."

"Stinking state that is."

"Perfectly awful."

"And then on to Wellesley."

"On to Wellesley."

"Like it there?"

"Certainly. It had a lot of class."

"What'd you major in?"

"What we talked about at lunch, art."

"Oh yeah, art. . . . What about you, Big One?"

"History," I said.

"That was my major, too."

"Good subject," I said, realizing too late it would stimulate his reflections upon it, and probably on education in general. Here, incidentally, I should warn you not to imagine that the terseness of Marjorie's and Giles's exchange reflected any particular antagonism between them. They were playing footsie with one another, grinning all the while. Listening to them riled me, but it didn't seem to bother Marjorie; and it certainly didn't bother Giles, at least not yet.

"It is a good subject. But I read what I wanted to read and never made Phi Beta Kappa. Only *arrivistes* go out for that anyway."

Jesus, I thought. *Arrivistes* again.

Now he lit a cigarette, an English Dunhill, let the smoke escape his mouth halfway, and sucked it in hoarsely. He seemed faintly emphysemic, and the inhalations and pauses were used to gather his energies for the longer deliveries which must follow. But a midwife was needed. Giles liked to think of himself as having been "drawn out."

"What did you want to read?" Marjorie asked.

"Serious?"

"Sure."

"OK. Among historical writers two stand out in my recollection, and I must confess to recurring to them with some frequency."

"Who?"

"Hegel and Polybius."

"*Who?*"

"Be pleasant, sweetheart," I told her.

"Hegel and Polybius. Also Nietzsche."

"What history did Nietzsche write?"

"Well, his historical works aren't of any great moment, but he had a few good points. The other two are much more significant figures in historical writing. Hegel I encountered when I was a freshman at Kansas State University, a citadel of learning at which you both may sneer, but which is staffed by a number of excellent intellectuals. One of them told me Marx had misused Hegel and had ruined Hegel's reputation in the process.

"Now this was only an obiter dictum dropped in private conversation, but it fired my imagination. I had already learned that the charlatan Marx had misused most people. And I thought to myself, here was a chance to see how he subverted the legacy of a great mind. So I read Hegel for myself. He had this theory called dialectical nationalism. It was like Toynbee, only Hegel's units of analysis were states instead of cultures. You can't have airtight cultures anyway, because they keep flowing into each other — for example, they've found pieces of Greek pottery on the ground outside a number of the pyramids, and you have that flow across the Alps in the last stages of the Renaissance, up into Holland and England. Charles the First, who this town fought for in the English Civil War, was really a Renaissance Prince. You can see the same thing in the play *Hamlet*, too, which is really about a neurotic who was also probably a homosexual maniac, how Shakespeare got his ideas for the plot-line from the Italian Mannerists. See?"

"That's a hell of a curriculum for an undergraduate."

But he ignored me and went on. "OK, after the rise of the nation-state as a viable unit you did have this dialectic like Hegel talks about. Say one state starts out weak, but its people are a hardy stock. They'll come back, they'll keep coming back until they've achieved their destiny. They rise and fall like a tide, but in the longer view they keep moving towards a crest. Look at Prussia. It was defeated by Napoleon, who wasn't even a full-blooded Gaul, and that defeat was a great stimulus to the German peoples. It brought them together in response to a common threat. And they went on to one success after another — Waterloo, Sedan, etcetera."

"On to the *führerbunker*."

"Mistress Quickly has a sharp tongue, Adams."

"My classy education, Mr. Giles."

She had got to him now. No veins popped out on his neck, and the American flag — worn this evening at his lapel — had not once been fingered. He was making all the Stations of the Cross: Eisenhower's defective pursuit, the genius of Douglas MacArthur, the unnecessary Vietnam quagmire, the native genius of Midwestern academia, the hateful Marx, rising and falling cultures, German resurgence. There was a good deal more to come, too, which I won't bore you with. In this particular harangue, his first of several, he concluded with the following law: "There is a great demiurge that controls the rise of states and their organizing principles."

"Sounds pretty bleak," I told him. "Determinist, almost."

"Not entirely. No — we've got Mistress Quickly here and Lady Godiva up at the bar. They relieve the tedium and make things bearable. Don't you, honey? . . ."

"I mean," Marjorie said, "is all this serious?"

"Very serious. And now, if you will excuse me . . ." and suddenly, as though setting out to prove something, he doubled his legs under him and bolted clumsily away from us, causing what was left of Marjorie's drink to slosh over the table and an ashtray to drop to the floor.

"Look what he's doing," Marjorie said.

"You put him up to it. I laid off him early . . ."

"No, look what he's *doing!*"

Giles had lurched the five or six steps to the bar and draped his arms like heavy wool scarves over the shoulders of the English couple standing there.

Almost at the same time his left hand came up — fingers joined and cupped like the head of a cobra — and dropped onto the top of the Englishman's head, while Giles looked, however, into the face of the young woman.

Could he know them? I shuddered, imagining his coarse breath in her face.

8

"I begyah pardon!" Giles didn't know him. "I begyah pardon, sir!"

I expected the Englishman would knock him out.

"Sir!" Giles popped to a quivering caricature of the military position of attention, slapping his arms against his trousers and clicking his heels. "Sir! I must say, your tattersall vest goes well with your stuffed shirt!"

I saw, with some disappointment, that there would be no violence. The Englishman saw only an American drunk, a bloody fool, a bounder. From his angle of vision I don't think he had seen Giles put his arm around the woman. He had little time to reflect, however.

"*Do* forgive me, sir," Giles entreated, "I mistook you for someone else, an old drinking companion from an earlier visit. Do forgive us." (With a gesture he included us in the plea.) "We should be honored if you'd join us at our table. Whadya say?"

"What an asshole," I said to Marjorie.

"You brought it all on. You stirred him up. And don't use that word."

"*I* brought it on?"

"You've made a career of doing that to people."

"We'll discuss it later."

Meantime the Englishman — the woman's uncle or whoever he was — had still said nothing, only fixed Giles with an outraged and unbelieving stare. Think about it. In the space of five seconds Giles had thrown his arm around his shoulders (something no adult had ever done to him, probably, since his boyhood nurse had steadied him in his bath), had performed the same offensive office on his lovely companion, had tousled his hair, had called him a stuffed shirt, had mocked his speech by bellowing "sir!" like a sergeant major . . . and had passed it all off as a case of mistaken identity.

Yet Giles was either cunning in his judgments or lucky. For the gentleman only steadied himself against the bar and in an uncertain, reedy falsetto voice demanded an apology.

None was forthcoming. Instead Giles pressed his invitation on them again. "Let me buy a drink, sir. You and the little lady."

They obeyed him. The Englishman signed for the little lady, the regular Joan Fontaine type not unlike those one saw in the audience at Broadway plays, to accompany him to our table. For reasons unknown? Unknown to me at the time, certainly. Later I would see and learn only too well that Frederick Giles exerted some strange compelling force on most people, particularly on people you would expect to be most repelled by him. He exuded a kind of magnetism he seemed able to intensify or dissipate at will. He was confident of it, too. In the 50's we called the type a "hot shit."

He was now very drunk. He staggered back to the Nelson Table and leaned on it like a wounded man while he got himself seated.

"I forget your name," he said to me.

"Big One, my name is Big One. And this is Mistress Quickly my wife."

"Howdoodo," mumbled the Englishman. He did not shake hands. They sat down.

In the course of the next few minutes, during which Giles said nothing, we learned our guest's name was Faricy and that he farmed some land out on the Barstow Pike west of Lawnsmere. Just now he was going in for pig farming, he said, pointing at his mixen-caked boots, and he had been in town late that afternoon to see a man on the business. All of which was meaningless, really, or at least very difficult to judge: half the English I know maintain they "farm some land" and they use the phrase as a synonym for "live in the country." But perhaps Faricy did. He looked like someone who lived close, but not too close to the soil: shabbily genteel in a way that suggested a certain contrivance, fingers knurled and stubby, an old something-or-other necktie.

And indeed the young woman was his niece. Faricy said her mother and father were abroad in Singapore; she had come to him on holiday from Benenden, a girls' school not far from London. Standing at the bar she had looked twenty-five. Across the table I saw she couldn't be more than eighteen. She had carried over a weak orange squash, and I heard her decline her uncle's offer of a gin to mix in it: "nothengiew." It was the only thing she said all night.

Philippa, as she was called, was right out of Thomas Hardy. She wore her impossibly thick and lustrous ash-blonde hair drawn severely back at the temples with a plain velvet hairband; it hung rich and shining over the back of her chair. Her face was narrow and her lips drawn slightly apart in an attitude of alert expectancy. She had also what Giles later saluted as a "really memorable set."

But there is no point in pressing the description further. For Giles, who now lay collapsed across the Nelson

Table, his head on his arm and his eyes vacantly focused on Marjorie like a small boy's watching a hated teacher — someone who was on to him — had dragged Faricy and his niece over to us only for use as props. They might as well have been manikins.

As though in some terrible spasm of pain he suddenly sat bolt upright, flung out his arm so that his fingers practically touched Philippa's set, and screamed: "Look at me, Marjorie! Look at me!"

She regarded him like a mother watching a child's tantrum.

"Now, goddammit, what do you make of this?"

"Make of what?"

"This, this!" With his forefinger he tapped at Philippa's collarbone. "Right here! *This* is what the hell it's all about. Can't you see that?"

Maybe Marjorie didn't, but I saw only too well what he was up to.

"This is where it's at! Not fucking Wellesley College or that East Coast shit you been feeding me all night. Princeton University, my ass! You come into this hotel and swank around so cool, put people on, get them talking . . . all the time you're snickering at them, laughing up your goddamned sleeve. You go up in your goddamned hotel room which I got you, goddammit, which *I* got you, otherwise Carstairs would have put you in some crummy room for the trash that stays here one night . . . you go up in your goddamned hotel room and say 'look at that fool spouting off all his right-wing bullshit, Jesus, what a stupid provincial, etcetera.' I know your type. Boy, do I know your type!"

He did, too, I thought.

"See," he said, now in a raspy quiet snarl, "This is

what the hell you think you are, but you aren't: you can't ever be like her, neither one a' you."

Philippa Faricy was unspoiled English beauty, grandly silent, unaffectedly modest, serene. In Giles's churning imagination, in his drunken paranoia, she had become a perfect and simple prop.

He was silent for a minute, making himself abject and ruminant for Philippa. "Madam," he said to her in a stage whisper, "allow me to fel-icitate you on the great beauty of your person — a person which, as your English writer Aldous Huxley once wrote, is far more than an opaque receptacle for the soul. Take a good look at her, Adams *et ux*, you can't ever be that."

The girl said nothing, only looked down at her lap and bit her lower lip.

It was easy to see what he was doing to us. His mental processes might be tortuous and bizarre, but we had clearly underestimated his sensitivity to ridicule. Now we were being paid back. We — but Marjorie in particular — had asked for it. Very well, he would seize the occasion to lash out at the things he hated, and which we — in the course of only an hour's drinking with him — had come to represent to him. "The effete East," I imagine he was thinking, who wanted to be like the English but couldn't do it to save their asses. The Wellesley Racket Club. The pansy mayor of Gotham. Phi Beta Kappa. Princeton University. Bomb them all into the Stone Age.

I apologized to Mr. Faricy.

"Apologize, bullshit! Faricy, you know what happened at this table?"

"I think so."

56

"Man sat there in eighteen-oh-five never apologized to anyone, now did he?"

"I daresay."

"Gentlemen and ladies, Lord Nelson!"

I lifted my glass, and Faricy, utterly bemused, his outrage perhaps salved by Giles's crude tribute to his niece, made as if to rise.

"Outta your goddamn chair, Adams."

"I believe the Royal Navy drill is to drink toasts sitting down."

"Alright, you siddown, I'll stand, dammit. This is one American not ashamed to toast an Englishman." He reeled crazily backwards, recovered himself, and drank. I hardly need add that most of his drink ran over the front of his shirt and his lapels.

A real sweetheart he was. And yet now, as suddenly as it began, the performance was over. Giles was groping about the admiral's table for his cigarettes and lighter, nodding like a penguin at each of us: "Good night, Madam. Good night, Uncle, Marjorie, Adams. Good night all of you."

"Oh, and Adams," he called from the hallway, "Did I ever tell you I hate those stinking foulard neckties?"

"Poor devil," Faricy said placidly.

Soon afterwards we followed him upstairs to our own room.

"What'd you make of that, Pleasant One?" I asked my wife.

"Shut up," she said. "Don't touch me, either."

9

I suppose a psychiatrist would have had a field day trying to make sense of what had just happened, the more so if he knew — as we did not — that these events would constitute the only encounter either of us was ever to have with a drunken Frederick Giles. After that night he stayed away from liquor pretty much, mainly because he must have thought — looking back on it — his behavior disgusted Marjorie. This, it transpired, was the last thing he wanted to do.

I also think he must have been in love with her right from the beginning. Her inaccessibility frustrated him; the few comments she had made while he rooted around in his ashheap of political and historical arcana enraged him, aggravated his frustration, and finally made him boil over. He did not do it again.

This should have been enough, you may think. During the rest of our stay in the Rufus all we had to do was avoid him, write off the unpleasantness as the result of a chance encounter with a boor and a slob.

Marjorie was not prepared to do that, however. "Be pleasant," she had said when I went to tinkering with him early in the evening. I had laid off him at once, and she had found herself taking up where I left off. A Bergdorf tuck-shop in the Wellesley gym, on to the *führerbunker*, and so on. Yet, despite the battering she had taken, she seemed consumed by remorse.

She was also drained by the experience. When she talked upstairs her voice was thin and quavering and I could hardly hear her. She sat at the edge of our bed, flipping her shoes at the closet in a listless underhand. She began rolling down her stockings, unaware — there was no question — of the terrible provocativeness of it. She knew I was watching her but went on with it with exquisite slowness. Now with both hands she reached down close to the floor, locked fingers over an ankle, and pulled her left leg up so that its heel was braced on the mattress against her buttock. Then she started rolling down the other stocking, and I moved towards her.

"Don't come near me," she said.

Yet she was too tired, too miserable, to sustain her anger.

"He really did us in, didn't he?" I heard her say.

"What's he to you? What the hell do you care?"

"You like to bait people, Mark. You like doing that. That's what kind of man you are."

I was watching Faricy and his niece down below on the street. They were walking in the direction of the only car parked on the High, Faricy clutching at Philippa's arm. A fine mist fell about them and Philippa held a newspaper over her head.

"You're guiltier than I am, Madam."

"No. I'm not cruel with people. You're cruel. You started him off."

"Nonsense. Hegel and Polybius. Nietzsche. Bullshit."

"You deserved it. Everything he gave you."

"He was giving it to you, not me. Mistress Quickly. The name rather suits you, you know."

"No, I wouldn't know."

She remained sitting on the edge of the bed, holding

her temples and staring at her feet. "I've got the curse," she said.

"I'm sorry."

"You're not sorry for me. You're sorry for yourself. Everywhere we go this awful egging people on. What are you trying to do to them? Don't you have anything better to do?"

"At the moment, yes. You don't have the curse."

"You're a bastard." She moved across the room in her slip and I studied the soft concavities at the sides of her buttocks, hollows, flesh. She threw her skirt at the chair and the chair toppled over.

"He's probably a kind man, you know. Confused and out of his depth."

"Are you kidding? What the hell's the matter with you?"

"He was very good with the children."

"The children."

"There're fifty million Gileses at home."

"Creatures of Hugh Hefner. They make me vomit. You catch those shoes he had on?"

"You're just as repulsive to him. He's crude, that's all."

"Never played squash rackets at Wellesley?"

"I was only kidding him."

"The hell you were."

"Did you wrap beetles in foil and burn them with matches as a boy?"

"You're a lovely piece of work yourself, Marjorie."

"What's the matter with us, Mark?"

"Don't make it a grade-B movie."

"Real tough guy, aren't you?"

We sank into the featherbed and I reached above us and found the light switch. Then I took her by the wrists and asked her if she were going to come quietly.

"Let the thing be pressed," she said, warming up and remembering an old joke between us.

10

I didn't bother to wake Marjorie the following morning. It was a warm fine day, almost balmy. Unexpected fragrances of autumn hung in the air and leaves stuttered about the High as I walked towards the station, stuttered and tumbled in shooting arcs in wayward updrafts. On either side of the street the half-timbered whitewashed Tudor buildings stood brightly in the sun, giving them the appearance of freshly made restorations for a movie set. In this tonic atmosphere I found myself keeping step with an Englishman fifteen or twenty yards ahead of me, a young slender father flanked by his two little girls.

The girls were dressed identically in blue gabardine overcoats worn shiny at the seat. Their blonde pigtails bobbed in counterpoint to their steps, jerked and bounced about as they half-walked, half-skipped to keep up with their father. He walked briskly and purposefully. He must get on with it. He must see about his business in town.

The girls also wore soft felt chapeaux—not beanies

exactly, but a sort of beret of Navy blue pulled tight over the crowns of their heads; and each beret had a little stem on top like an applestem. Diagonally, across their backs, frizzled khaki straps clamped little canvas receptacles close to their right sides: their "kit." I thought of those WREN officers you saw in World War II movies, striding through the pigeons into the Admiralty.

The father talked to them as they hurried along, accentuating his remarks with odd woodpecker-like movements of his head. After each utterance the little girls giggled and sobered quickly in a sort of controlled bumptiousness — the effect produced being one of a certain hothouse primness. They *would* be good! At this point Papa deposited them at a bus shed set back from the sidewalk, said something I could just make out about Father Christmas, patted them on the backs and kissed them in dry darting pecks. I reckoned he must be a clerk of some sort.

"Off you go!" he said. Off they went, scurrying for a seat on the bench inside. By the time I drew abreast both girls were seated, tight together, and studiously rifling through the pages of hard-backed schoolbooks: looking for a fact, getting things down just right.

Eight or nine years old, these two. Other girls stood around the bus stop on the curb, girls somewhat — and in a couple of cases much — older than the first two. One of them might have been seventeen; she was certainly tall enough, but it was difficult to judge figures under those coats, and I had a notion that they wore some kind of mashing bra that kept them flat until they finished school. This tall one was dressed exactly like the others, with the exception that she wore black stockings instead of floppy gray socks. She was not wearing makeup.

"Hi, there, you-all," I said to them generally. The tall one looked at me surprised and — it seemed — somewhat wounded. Like a graceful young doe she stood apart from the others. She raised her chin slightly just as I was walking past her and said "hello" in a wonderfully clear chorister's voice. A lovely child-woman as I say: dewy, pale, perfectly assured. Delicate pilasters of white-gold hair hung before her ears and her hands were clasped behind her back. "Hello."

She was lovely, but she had not really seen me. Her eyes had followed me briefly, but they had looked beyond me, almost as though I represented something she knew to be contemptible and threatening. In any case she must get on with it, too, must see about her business. She was going straightaway to do her Livy and then straightaway to marry the Hon. R. H. H. Boadley-Leigh, let us say, and then directly on to fetch the groceries in her Mini-Minor and her nappies and to drink one dry vermouth at the district manager's house in Godalming. He would be her husband's boss. She would love her husband very much, he would possess her completely, and he would look like Leslie Howard.

Neither you nor Giles will ever touch her, Adams: no American. No North American fighter pilot with his fifty-mission crush and his briny tarnished wings on his tunic ever got to her mother in War Two and none of you will get to her now. You can't touch these women; and if you did they wouldn't notice you. It was a bitch.

I arrived at the station and stopped at the newsstand to buy a paper. Soon the engineless train came sliding and clicking at us all standing there reading. I got on and took my hangover into a first-class compartment and tried to read.

I could not read. All I could think about was Giles last night, what he had shouted at Marjorie and what she, in the strange access of compassion and remorse which seized her from time to time in situations not unlike these, had said of him in our room. It was as though she was saying Giles was a better man than me: better an honest outraged boor than an intolerant cynic out to amuse himself by baiting a new acquaintance. It was as though she felt his savage ridicule was something we both had earned and deserved, and that, if we gave the man our understanding and friendship, he would prove — as she already felt him to be — more than worthy of it.

I didn't know. Was it disgust for me, loathing for herself, some unbelievable attraction to Giles? "Broads respond to that shit, you know," a friend you will meet later used to say to me. When he got really drunk he would compare women to rattlesnakes: "The only way to handle them is to grab their ass by the tail and twirl them around your head, around and around, and then snap them up like a whip. They calm down fast that way."

Well . . . But Marjorie is nothing if not her own woman. She has had a history of seeing things in lights different from mine, and you should hear some of it before I go any further.

TWO

Marjorie

11

I met Marjorie Semple in the Yale Co-op in August, 1963. I stood behind her in a line at the check-out counter, and while she was sorting through her change with enough deliberation to make me think she wanted to meet me, I asked the cashier if there were a copy of Lucretius' *De Natura Rerum* in the store. "Who the hell do you think I am?" he answered with practiced insolence, "Bernard De Voto?" In 1963, as always, New Haven abounded in smartasses. And before I could formulate a suitable comeback (De Voto never picked his nose on duty, something like that), Marjorie had looked up from her purse, spun around to face me and said, "Lucretius, come on!" as a child might say "Maravich better than Clyde Frazier? Come on!" — said it in a voice so willful and so arch it practically froze me. At the same moment, as if on command, the books I had been carrying slipped out of my arms to the floor and she bent down at once to help me pick them up, announcing their titles as she saw them, commenting on them one by one: "Gee, do you read that?" and "Gosh" and "How about that?" Perhaps you remember the expression Eisenhower had on his face when he was told Truman had fired MacArthur. Her voice captured that expression, more or less: surprised, bemused, not altogether displeased. But I soon saw she was clowning for the benefit of two bluestockings with whom she had been shopping, and I noticed at the same time the faint smell of beer on her breath: "*Sch*pengler," she said, emphasizing the *Sch*, "do you read him? Sorokin, what is that, like seborrhea? Cecil Woodham-Smith, you read him?"

"Her," I triumphantly caught her. "Her. It's a woman." The ladies tittered.

"Big deal," said Marjorie, "a genuine summertime scholar."

We have been married nine years now, but I remember that meeting as though it had been this morning, and probably because Marjorie's comments revealed in that moment a nuance in her personality I was to notice only occasionally again for many months; and because, though she now sneers constantly at my books and my research studies, she rarely betrayed in our courtship or in the first year or two of our marriage any such attitude towards them except in the vagrancies of jest. Why had she done it then, I still wonder — snickered, perhaps even sneered at me? Had she drunk too much at lunch? She drinks almost nothing. And she was, and remains, the most tolerant of women.

I recovered quickly enough and asked her to have coffee with me, excusing us from her friends on the grounds they should be spared the pedantries of anyone who read Sorokin. They went off with a bad grace and Marjorie and I left the Co-op together.

In those days I must have been an obnoxiously serious student of English history. I had done a year's work (or, I had better say, had a year's soak) at Cambridge as a Taliaferro scholar, and had come home that summer to work under Dr. Paul Merry, a distinguished constitutional historian who had been an honorary fellow of my college. He had a grant to work at Yale — a grant and a commission to put in order a valuable manuscript collection given the University by the American widow of an English marquess recently deceased. I spent my days as his research assistant.

Dr. Merry loved his work and thought it important; I hated it and thought it a waste of time. I was tempted more than once to ask him what Edmund Wilson said it was always fun to ask scholars: That sort of thing really interest you? But I never did. The marquess had been a war poet, a very bad one but a contemporary of Owens and Sassoon. He had written the bulk of his verse between the ages of eighteen and twenty-four, and it seemed somehow monstrous to me that Dr. Merry was "working on" them, a seventy-year-old constitutional historian with a grant. But he was a friend of the marquess' wife.

I spent my days carrying books and papers to him, up to his smoky carrel in the stacks of Sterling Library where he sat with a bookie's shade pulled over his nose, over his desiccated scholar's face and its yellowed moustaches. He is the last academic I have seen who, literally, wore strings around the arms of his shirt.

Evenings I stayed out in Woodbridge at the house of some old friends of my mother's. This was a summer for serious, even ardent reading. Before Cambridge my knowledge of my subject had come mainly out of smug and fruity modern histories of England, all of them written by Americans from places like Ball State; these, and from paperback collections of "excerpts" bearing titles like *William I: Hero or Villain?* Of English history in the grand manner I was almost wholly ignorant, except for Churchill's *History of the English-Speaking Peoples* which, I had been told at Princeton, was "not scholarly."

My tutor at Cambridge had found me out quickly. "Had a go at 'contemporary civileyezation,' have you, in America? This is what you cawl history in New Jersey, I believe?" I chuckled in appreciation, but he was not trying to be funny. "Read Macaulay? No? Not read Macaulay? Incredible! Get to him at once, sir, at once! Not read Lewis Namier? — an historian of the first quality! Read him, sir, read him through! And Acton?"

"A little, I think," I answered, terrified he would press for particulars, but he did not, thank God.

"Well, yes, quite right, only wrote a little, quite right. Froude?"

"No, sir."

"Maitland? Stubbs? Robertson? Hume? Gibbon? Covell?"

"A little Covell, I think."

"No such man, do not trifle with me, sir." He paused to sip at his tea. "The Shakespeare history tetralogies? — do not sneer at those, sir, do not sneer at them. Imaginative reconstructions of a largely unknown past are not to be sneered at. That is your art! Shall you be a 'slight unmeritable man, meet to be sent on errands'?"

"No, sir."

"Then you must read, lad. Read things through! Never read Smollett? Sterne? Richardson? Fielding? Dickens?"

" 'A Christmas Carol.' "

" 'Christmas Carol,' indeed. See to it, sir. See to your reading! Do me a paper on the Norman Conquest and feudalism. Off you go!"

Off I went from my first tutorial, by now conscious that the don was a "character" and perhaps not to be taken seriously. I saw to very little of what he told me to, at least not during my first year at the University. Instead I saw to North Devon, to Ely Cathedral, to the Royal Festival Hall, to Paris and Copenhagen, to every copy of *Encounter,* to Joyce and Eliot, to Trevor-Roper and Ved Mehta. How did one drink from a fire hydrant, anyway? It was all I could do to "get up" my essays each week: Had Aristotle an Ideal State? Can Men Be Forced To Be Free? What Did the Berlin Congress Settle? Did Columbus Go Too Far?

It turned out Mr. Westmacott was very serious indeed, however, and I was left with a staggering list of books to read the summer when I met Marjorie. I was errand-boy to a dryasdust during the day, a Wolfeian reader at night. I flogged myself to do three or four hundred pages each evening between dinner and bedtime. "Drink deep draughts, read them through," the don had said. "Read things whole!"

Graduate students did not quail at such prospects in 1963; in fact there was some exhilaration in reading what one had been told to read. Do you remember the time? Of Jacqueline Kennedy, of John Glenn, of cropped heads and students who, if they were as arrogant as they are now, nonetheless turned their arrogance on different things — books and scholars for example, not treaties with Asian countries and college presidents? But one could read Macaulay's rhythmic swelling sentences, could applaud his comparisons of London in the time of Charles II to the wild jungles populated by the ignorant savages of Dahomey: progress, optimism, certitude — they had a familiar and easy resonance with our own outlook. Black was only the color of a good-looking car in 1963, the color of the limousines, for example, that carried Mr. Rostow and Dr. Schlesinger to the White House each morning, confidently to assist their president in the governance of a liberal democracy. Riots were for Latin American soccer stadiums, assassinations for places like Bechuanaland.

Indeed, one immersed oneself in the humane letters with much joy and little irony.

I was not looking for romance that summer, but Marjorie Semple took me like a seizure. I found myself helpless around her, shaky and weak. She was calm, sure, indulgent. She was working too — a summer student from Wellesley doing art history. That first afternoon she invited me to a seminar on the *Fauves*. I learned some things about her.

Fifteen students sat behind a long table facing a portable movie screen, all of them young women except for a couple of airy-fairies who gasped each time a new painting was projected onto it. You must know the routine: slide projector angled up off a couple of encyclopedia volumes, violently enthusiastic art professor pacing up and down the side of the room with a remote mechanism clutched in his hand like a grenade, blotches of primary colors appearing on the screen like ketchup packages exploding on the shirts of Hollywood bandits, everyone smoking like crazy . . .

"And what of this?" he would say.

Bryn Mawr would answer him: "Oh, it's lovely, it's sort of, sort of . . . worn and etiolated. Look at the tree trunks. That marvelous gunmetal pigmentation! What wonderful contrasts! He must have worked in Rouault's *atelier!*"

Gush like this, lots of it. Every other phrase was "sort of." The art students had an obnoxious habit of enunciating their words as though they were trying to go to the bathroom as they said them; and they spoke in a kind of academic English accent — Ronald Coleman and the Halls of Ivy come to mind — a dangerous way to talk in which the American speaker winds up in bêtises like putting ashes in the awshtray.

The professor was pleased with Bryn Mawr. "Very well articulated, Rosea, well done. Marjorie?"

Marjorie's responses ran to the languid. She saw the silliness of the exercise. "Marjorie passes," she said.

"Erich?" said the professor, superciliously. He was not gratified by the tone of Marjorie's answer. "Ed-dich?"

"It's like a boxcar standing on its end in a siding. So tactile! So, sort of, pal-pable."

"Very good indeed. Now the construction of the picture will repay our scrutiny. Marney?"

And there followed more prattle about musculature and articulating and defining space. There were some real howlers. One of the lightfeet described the texture of a Kandinsky as "crepuscular."

But by this time I was not listening to them or looking at the paintings. I was looking at Marjorie, sitting by myself at the end of the table, watching her gestures and studying her face in the irradiations playing over it from the screen. She was exquisite in profile: she had an unusually high forehead, delicately veined at the temples; thick auburn hair carelessly arranged in a coif; a long nose, impossibly straight and finely molded at the nostril; very full lips — the lower lip scalloped slightly downward, strangely quivering from time to time as Marjorie looked at the pictures, a child-like feature which made me wonder what she had looked like as a little girl.

I loved her serenity, her amused tolerance, her patience with the idiot enterprise going on around her, her gentle ironic laughter, which she kept up as a kind of forgiving *obligato* to the frantic nonsense of the student critics.

I loved her too for the calmness of her gestures: for the way she put the tips of her reading glasses to the corners of her mouth and quietly smoothed her hair; and perhaps most of all for the fact that she never looked at me during the two hours we were together in that seminar. No gimcrack preening or nervous laughter; no conspiratorial winking — Isn't this absurd? Aren't they ludicrous — though in a moment of dread I saw this might be because Marjorie credited me with no more sense than her fellow students. Who was I to her, anyway?

From time to time the tip of her tongue would touch at her upper lip, absently, a dreamy and innocent gesture almost child-like; and as she sat listening to the professor — still pacing about like a caged panther — she would trace with her fingers the pale down along her jaw.

Marjorie is a tall woman, strongly boned and heavily bosomed, something she seemed to try to hide. If I had not fallen in love with her I would have described her then as a ripe specimen, a woman quietly smoldering under the armory of nondescript bulky blouses and sweatshirts she wore. But this would have been inaccurate. She seemed so perfectly self-possessed and untroubled, so unconscious of the unconcealable beauty of her person that I felt somehow chastened when I was around her.

Two days after the slide show my mother's friends left Woodbridge on vacation, leaving me alone in their house. I brought Marjorie out for dinner that night and made us a clumsy dinner of lamb chops and baked potato, self-conscious under her amused inspection to the point of dropping the potatoes on the floor. I sensed she saw me as gawky and foolish, and that whatever appeal I had for her was to some unknown maternal instinct in her character. Partly out of artifice I settled into the role I imagined she wanted me in. At this stage I would have done anything to please her.

After dinner I read to her from Gibbon's *Autobiography*: the gentle pathetic passage in which the historian takes his everlasting leave of his old and agreeable companion, his history of the *Decline and Fall*. Her response, no different from what it would be now nine years later, was to ask me if I enjoyed being force-fed: "like a male suffragette doing penance," she said. I grasped at the chance not only to show her how much I loved Gibbon, which I did, but also I think to indemnify myself against what might come later. What was ingenuous was forgivable; what was artifice was not. I wanted to sleep with her. If later I took her in my arms and she pulled away from me I wanted to convince her that it was for love I did it, that it was "natural," that that night — the dinner and talk and reading — had no plan, no artifice behind it.

I wanted to indemnify myself as we all did with our first great loves, by exalting sex, by lifting it out of the ruck of carnal life and its strange persistent identification with shame, by resolving our uncertainties about the responses of those we love by being able to show that it was, after all, pure passion that had led us to where we were, and that passion sometimes entails irresponsible behavior.

The Gibbon was restrained and elegant. I was foolish. Gibbon was as unnecessary to my purposes as the art seminar had been to Marjorie's. I lay the book down.

"He's conceited, that Gibbon. A peacock like you."

12

Later, in the long and gradual dissipation of our love, she would say such things more and more often, nasty deflating comments issued to wound. Now she seemed only irritated, but indulgently so, and I loved her for it. I reached out to her, and she kissed the palm of my hand.

There was a great summer storm gathering outside. I stood and brought her up next to me and kissed her. We heard the eaves and shutters clattering as the wind came up, so perfectly timed that it made us both laugh, and we went upstairs together.

She stood in my jersey beside a window and I came up behind her and took her in my arms; and for a long time we watched the storm thicken, saw it become unbearably opaque and heavy and sundered finally by lightning breaking jaggedly from its depths. Below in the meadow the wind cut ripples in the tall grass, wavering fan-vaultings which seemed to freeze in the sharp explosions of light, freeze and vanish and reappear magically in new patterns. The wind soughed heavily in the huge maples near the window and spray rasped over us as it blew the rain across the screen. I kissed her neck and her ears and felt my hands huge and strong over her belly. In that time I worshipped Marjorie, and before dawn she hung above me and the fullness of her hair hid us away from the storm, now finally retreating away towards the coast.

For the next three weeks of nights and days we lived together in Woodbridge, guessing nervously at the date of the Wallachs' return and using only one bed in their guest room. We didn't need to worry on this account, as Marjorie was not to meet them until our marriage next summer. I don't think our work suffered by our living together, either, if by her reluctant study of modern painting what she was doing might qualify as work. She continued to spend her mornings in seminars. Much as she disliked them, they would give her a certain number of credit hours and more freedom during her last year at Wellesley.

We did other things together. One cruelly hot Sunday afternoon we drove up to Tanglewood to hear Claudio Arrau play the Brahms D-Minor Piano Concerto, a dark raging hymn of despair which has haunted me since my mother first played it for me and which I now wished to share with Marjorie. There was depth and richness to the texture of our love, but our interests were divergent, or rather what we seemed to value in the arts had little in common.

It was no soft sell I gave her, either about Brahms or Leinsdorf and Arrau; nor was I sensitive to her responses.

In fact it was more than a month from then before I saw she could be forced to like nothing unless it were in reponse to some errant impulse of her own. And on this Sunday, to complicate things more, I had foolishly invited two members of her seminar to come with us, and they and I argued all the way up about romantic music generally and about the piano concerto we were going to hear. Marjorie's friends brandished words like bludgeons: tonalities, *tuttis,* modulations. Neither of them listened to the other, or to Marjorie, who said very little. One of the two friends, Marney, whom I thought Marjorie liked, finally began dominating the conversation: now talking about structure, now about the "disappointing, irresolute rondo," now insisting Brahms be fixed in his proper Teutonic context, that his personal life was important to any meaningful discussion of his music. He had for example written the concerto in its original form under the ghastly shadow of Schumann's suicide gesture and his terrible breakdown.

I had never heard any of this and said so.

"Oh, it's all in Tovey," Marney answered.

I asked her how Schumann tried to kill himself.

"By jumping off a bridge into the Rhine River," she said.

"I'll jump out of the car if you don't shut up," Marjorie cried.

I had never really seen her angry. Now she was sallow with rage and a thin perspiration had broken out above her mouth. She did not look at us, and when I reached across the seat to touch her, she brushed my hand away. She had screamed at Marney as though pushed beyond some unknown limit of rage.

"You're an ass, Marney. You're no more capable of

loving a picture or a concerto than a computer is. They've ruined you."

Nobody answered her. When I tried to give her a dollar to give the parking attendant, she pushed my hand away again, with a certain repugnance that told me what she had said to Marney was meant for me, too.

An hour later we were sitting inside the great shed, five or six rows back from the stage. Soon Leinsdorf made his way through the players to his conductor's stand, smiled his brusque gamin's smile at the audience and nodded to Arrau. The music began, bleak and mesmerizing, flowing and gathering into the great unhurried amplitudes of most of Brahms's orchestral music. After a few minutes the pianist bent down to the work, and at the first quiet annunciation of his theme Marney plopped open the heavy pages of a score she had brought with her, found her place, and began miming the motions of the pianist. I looked for Marjorie's reaction to this; she was sitting primly, straight-backed between Marney and me.

The pages turned and the comments began — Marney's comments, whispered to the other girl we'd brought with us, but quite audible to everyone. "He's taking it too slow," she said breathlessly: "Too slow . . . there's a clinker . . . E sharp . . . rubato! . . . he'll ruin the cadenza."

Marjorie: "It has no cadenza, Marney. This concerto has no cadenza. You're a bigger fraud than I thought you were." She took the score off Marney's lap and placed it quietly on the floor and put her feet on it.

I saw only too clearly that Marjorie's fine rage *was* aimed at me, not at this dowdy friend of hers, who was probably either inured to such behavior or strong enough not to let it bother her much. In her eyes perhaps what Marjorie had done appeared to be some sisterly bullying. I looked at Marney and tried to reassure her that I understood about Marjorie, and I remember being shaken to find the same expression on Marney's face, looking at me.

The swirling rondo, which Leinsdorf and Claudio Arrau executed at dizzying and dangerous speed, brought the audience screaming out of their seats, made them applaud wildly. But Marjorie said only: "Had enough?" She gave no time for an answer, but picked up her purse and her friend's score and walked up the aisle. She was out of the shed before we caught her.

Just as suddenly the whole thing passed off. She never apologized. She never even mentioned the incident. But that night for the first time she arranged our lovemaking, set its conditions and tone, and loved me with an abandon that put Brahms in grave doubt.

13

The summer wore quietly away. I understood that Marjorie felt she had made her point at the concert, and that she was satisfied I saw what that point was: We might be in love, but whatever we shared was not to be desecrated and ruined by anything intellectual or academic. As long as I kept my enthusiams to myself — in music, in art, in literature — and as long as I didn't try to force them on her, I was safe. Marjorie believed that things felt along the heart demanded to be utterly private and must remain inarticulable: "We murder to dissect." To gush about something one had read or saw or heard was to ruin it; to gush cleverly like the critics of art and language was to destroy their very soul, to ruin the joys they had been created to give.

But I did not learn my lesson well enough. The day before I flew back to England with Dr. Merry, Marjorie and I went to Hartford to look at an exhibition of modern art which her seminar had visited earlier that summer. I was now on far more treacherous grounds than I knew. My tastes in painting have always been unsettled and unformed; but from what I could learn from Marjorie's disappointed comments about her seminar, I had somehow gotten the notion that she thought most modern painting a terrible sham, an organized collection of jokes foisted on a public too uncertain of its tastes to reject it.

I followed her patiently through the galleries of the Wadsworth Atheneum, watching her walk, mainly, and not looking at the pictures; nodding agreement at her few curt judgments and asking questions about technique — questions as innocent-sounding as I could possibly make them. She had said it was one of those museums that have a lot of juvenalia and lesser-known works by famous artists, including several from her period; nothing much good, although every now and then an unexpected jewel would turn up. But for the two hours we walked through the humid galleries she said nothing to make me think she had found one of these.

Finally, in the last room we walked through, Marjorie stopped and stared. A great gray canvas with a maroon border and a small sphere in the bottom left-hand corner had been hung recently; she had not seen it before. The sphere on close inspection turned out to be a basketball, and the painting bore the cryptic title *K-37*. I told Marjorie the title sounded like a dog food or some peak in the Andes and that the picture was trash. Anyone could have done it. She pointed at a white card attached to the bottom of the frame, and "anyone" turned out to be a Joachim Halperin, a freshman at the Rhode Island School of Design; the painting had just been awarded first prize in an annual competition for younger New England artists.

I told Marjorie again the painting was silly, and looking back on it, it seemed a perfectly safe thing to say. I had the notion she thought such tripe as contemptible as I did. Still she said nothing. She walked slowly back and forth in front of the thing, sometimes stopping and putting her face up close to the canvas, then stepping back, fanning herself with her guide.

"He can't even draw a basketball," I said.

"Shut up," she said. "Shut up. Let's get in the car." She wheeled about and strode bristling through the galleries, veering away from me each time I caught up to her.

All the way home I pleaded with her. I was sorry. I was stupid. I was a barbarian, I didn't know anything about art. Come to think of it, the picture was magnificent — eloquently simple, the best thing I'd seen all summer. I told her my first impressions of paintings were always wrong.

This time she didn't tell me to shut up. All she said was that I should keep the car running when we got to

Woodbridge so that she could run in and get her things. "Then drop me off in town."

"You can't go through life acting like this," I finally said to her. "There're people who love you and you've got to explain yourself to them."

"Don't whimper at me."

I reminded her it was our last night together for a long time, and that she was ruining everything, our whole summer.

But of course this only made things worse, so I said nothing more until we stopped in front of her apartment in New Haven. By the time I had come around to her side of the car she had jumped out and was running away up the walk, pushing and slapping at the air like a child: gestures of repugnance so frantic and determined that I figured the incident in the gallery couldn't possibly have set her off by itself, and that her anger had been building up for some time.

She got to the door and into the hall before I could stop her, and she locked the door behind her.

"Please, Marjorie, for God's sake!"

"You heard what I said, Mark," she said.

I heard her go up the stairs and then another door slammed. I had heard what she said, alright: "Shut up." I did. I did not call her that night, and by the time my outrage had subsided and yielded to a sorrow so heavy and terrible that I could feel it in the palms of my hands and in my throat — by then — I was halfway across the Atlantic, on my way back to Cambridge.

14

In times of grief one's consciousness registers and stores in sharp outline and detail incidents and conversations utterly unconnected with the anguish or its causes. The plane going back to England was practically empty; I remember its atmosphere as chilly and clean and bright, and I remember sitting back against the window with my legs stretched across the vacant adjoining seats. I was reading, or rather trying to read, *Tristam Shandy*, thinking at once how indefatigable a scholar I was, how dense and vital were these chapters of Sterne's, and how Marjorie would have laughed her lilting deprecatory laugh to see me conning, rather than enjoying (she would assume) what I was reading. I was thinking these things when I heard a male voice above me say, "Do you mind?" As I swung my legs to the floor to make way for the passenger I heard the voice say, "Look at this, will you," and saw him sit down in the aisle seat next to me.

He held out the front page of an English tabloid, and its headline said SOCCER STAR WEDS.

"Look at that woman. Recognize her?"

I said I didn't think so.

"Y'know who it is?" he asked. "It's Debra Dorfmann. Y'know who she is? Best singer in London. Y'know who she was married to before? The Earl of Halesworth. Now look at this bloke." He thrust the paper close to me; his hands were shaking and smelled of cologne. "Bloody football player."

I looked at the athlete, a curly haired, high-cheek-boned young man with a carnation in his lapel. His face wore a vacant bovine expression, as though he didn't know where he was. Across his waist his forearm lay stiffly; his fingers, fat and knobby-knuckled, extended together to the edge of his coat. Debra Dorfmann's hand was hung over the crook of his arm, and in the background were three or four beer mugs held aloft by disembodied hands. It was a scene of some squalor, and rather ludicrous.

"Now why would *she* marry someone like this?"

"I can't imagine," I said.

"You want to know why?"

"Why?"

He leaned close to me to whisper and I saw he wore a cat's-eye ring on his forefinger. "Why?" I asked him again.

"Because he had a big one. That's the only explanation." The man smacked his lips. Then he disappeared, as suddenly as he had sat next to me.

15

Presumably Marjorie went to her family in Far Hills for the next couple of weeks, and then back to Wellesley. I did not hear from her, and it wasn't for several months that I heard anything about her. All through a damp autumn the recollection of our precious nights together haunted me, an impossible shadow in a sunless world. There were moments when I thought I saw her in the flocks of gowned undergraduates rushing along the streets after lectures, leaning together into the wind; and I would stop and wait for her shape to detach itself from the crowd. Twice I imagined that I distinguished her from the rest, that she was suddenly standing alone as the mass retreated beyond her. She was standing alone before Trinity Great Court, lifting up her arms in a kind of yearning, supplicatory recognition, beckoning silently for me to come to her as my mother had beckoned me to her bed the night she heard of my father's death. "Marjorie?" I would say quietly, treasuring the sound of her name, moving slowly towards her, waiting for the vision to vanish as I knew it must, later finding myself in the warmth of a bookstore being asked for the third time if I could be helped. But I could not be.

Except that by December, in early December in the bleakest of my days at Cambridge, bereft of friendships I had ruined by my self-pitying misery — all of them but my flatmate David Ashley's — except that by then the great wound was slowly beginning to heal. And it healed as a bruise does, becoming ugly in the process.

I grew cynical. I no longer wrote Marjorie. She had answered none of my letters, letters which, because I sensed any restatement of my "case," anything that she might take for whimpering, could only make things worse. I began to set bottoms to my sadness, envisioning the worst possible things she might do to me. Though I could not quite imagine her acting vindictively, I could just see her marrying.

That was it, I decided: she had married. In three years she would be driving to the station in Haverford or Cos Cob with two squalling infants beside her in the front seat, the backs of her knees hideously varicosed, her belly creased and soft; driving to pick up some natty J. Press of a broker for whom (since he would have read nothing, heard no music, looked at no paintings, recited no poetry since he had left the Hill School) unsafe articulations of feeling and criticisms of "art" would be impossible.

That was it. Marjorie would become the quiet, compliant, sustaining half of an "attractive young couple." She would roll Ace bandages at the Junior League and mail them to Pakistan. She would hide her sagging breasts in the folds of a flowered Lilly. She would lie in bed on a Sunday morning with Press Junior, drinking her Tang and reading advertisements in the *Times Magazine*.

And therefore the hell with her. David and I stopped studying and started going to parties night after night. I grew a beard and drank Campari before lunch and slept around. For a while I forgot her.

In February I had a letter from a Princeton classmate at Harvard Law School whom Marjorie had met the previous summer in New Haven. "Old Artificer," it began:

> Now this a nasty little operation they have here. I have an ulcer and my teeth and hair are falling out. My eyesight is failing and you can see from the jaggedness of my penmanship what the grind is doing to me. I study for eight hours, drink for four, sleep six, study eight . . . it is wearing and I wish I was you. And all this for ten grand a year and a stinking desk at Sullivan Cromwell — who interviewed me last week in New York, where I also saw that astoundingly gorgeous? ex-friend of yours in Jimmy Ryan's bar with some little Playboy Club type with his arms all over her. What was her name — Natalie? Marjorie? Can't remember. Not that I gave a rat's ass, or you either. She looked pendulous and her friend was all over her. Must be better

for you in England, where the females are all staid and you have
to turn them on — right? When do you graduate from there?

And early in March:

> . . . and saw Marjorie again, this time at a party a girl gave in
> Southborough, Marjorie with the same rodent-like nonentity as
> before, a singularly offensive, greasy type, like a bowling cham-
> pion or a flyweight division contender. He was about 5′ 4″ and
> she's what?, 5′ 10″? and his schnazola comes up about to her
> cleavage. What a woman like that would see in a clod like this
> I can't imagine, but it'll make you glad you got out (as it were)
> when you did. See you.

I said nothing in answering these letters to make
Crawford think what he had written bothered me. If I
had done this — my thinking ran — he would have
wound up defending my interests, which would either
have made things irreparably worse, or which would
have led to his falling for her. Better to have her sleeping
with whomever it was than Crawford. But it was painful
enough, the more so as I knew I should not write her;
and because I knew I would be taking my life in my
hands if I ever brought it up with her later, if I ever
saw her again.

In those days I had an interesting notion about girls.
I reckoned they were alright if they slept with two men.
More than this — well, then things would get messy and
complicated. Two was the limit of unpromiscuous behavior. Ricardo or whoever he was made two. If she
stopped there, things weren't hopeless. It was a rebound,
a *jeu d'esprit*, a fling. Perhaps she was still safe.

My friend's letters had given me twinges of grief, but
whatever little agonies they provoked were salved by
rationalizations like the one I've just mentioned; and by

the coming of a spring like all Cambridge springs, a time of soft frolics and dewy dawns and languor, and of the bittersweet realization that I was never to live through a Cambridge spring again. I found myself able to walk, with a disappointed but resigned lover's equanimity, through the rich carpets of late daffodils and crocuses in the Backs, over Trinity Bridge and through the gateway at Christ's. I could hear the choir at King's singing Palestrina and Elgar in the twilight, could lie in a punt looking up at the gentle fleece of clouds with a book of Hopkins open on my chest, hearing the gorpy suck of the pole being thrust behind me — could do all these things in the loveliest and most fragrant place in the world without a thought of Marjorie Semple. Without a twinge, even.

In May I had to abandon my meager preparations for the exams that loomed ahead in six weeks. My first step-father, by all accounts a decent soul, but who had not lasted long enough for me to know him well, had, according to the telegram, "suffered massive coronary thrombosis and passed on to his reward funeral Tuesday."

I flew to New York and called Marjorie as soon as the plane landed.

16

A young woman's voice, in that chilling tone of boredom and irritation you might associate with undergraduates in a women's college, told me to hold on. I imagined

Marjorie unhurriedly sauntering down a dim peeling hallway in a terry-cloth bathrobe, thinking she would have to deal with some horny courtier, perhaps her bowling champion.

"Marjorie Semple," she said, "Who's this, please?"

I asked her if I'd caught her writing me a letter.

"Hello, darling. I miss you terribly."

I couldn't make out whether she was being sarcastic.

"I do," she said. "Where are you, darling, in England?"

"No, Idlewild."

"Idlewild Airport?"

"Yes."

"Should I come down there?"

I couldn't believe what I was hearing. I asked her if she were serious.

"Of course I'm serious. Is your mother at her apartment now?"

"No, she's in Wilmington." So much for the funeral. I heard the muffled crackle of a hand pressed over the receiver, and several interrogative noises.

"Can you meet me in LaGuardia? In three hours?"

"But all those months, Marjorie," I said. "No letters, no news, nothing."

"No cross-examinations — right?"

"Anything you say."

But already she had put the receiver back.

We had three days together in New York. Nothing was changed from last summer, nothing at all, and in the early evenings when I lay watching the play of branches reflected on the pale green ceiling of my mother's guest room, and I thought of asking Marjorie about the year that had passed between us, I rejected the notion. I had learned my lesson.

Two months later she was pregnant; and I, having "satisfied the examiners, and having been placed by them in the lower half of the Second Class," which showed I had not satisfied them too well — I took my leave of the University of Cambridge and came home to marry Marjorie.

17

We were married in Routledge, the placid village in western Connecticut where my mother has lived for some years, married on a warm September afternoon in 1964 by the Very Reverend Harmon Johnson, Bishop of southwestern New England, in the Church of St. James Protector. I remember sitting in the tiny sacristy, looking out at the congregation through a crack in the doorway. I entertained myself by counting the number of men who had worn madras coats to the ceremony. Madras coats were just barely alright that year, but only if they were worn with black trousers; and if you really wanted to be stylish, they could be worn with formal trousers and you could wear patent leather dancing pumps with them. From the sacristy I could see that Page Connell, the Philadelphia attorney, had done so. His legs were crossed, and a dangling shoe shone like a mirror in the slanting afternoon sunlight.

The wedding was dominated by a too determined solemnity. We had, for instance, hired an accomplished organist, a Mr. Dietrich Münchler who had retired from St. George's Church in Hartford only that summer. I had gotten my mother to offer him five hundred dollars to transcribe the third movement of the Dvořak Seventh Symphony and play it for Marjorie's processional, but at the last moment he had had to beg off, owing to an "unobliging prostate," and the local girl who took his place managed only a watery Buxtehude prelude and the usual ruck of Wagner and Mendelssohn. Yet I was grateful even for that, after hearing her try to accompany a local schoolboy in the Purcell Trumpet Voluntary (sometimes assigned to Jeremiah Clark) on the morning of the wedding.

My little cousin Pringle Smith dropped the ring in handing it to my best man. Tears fell like seed pearls from the eyes of my mother. An usher somehow stepped on Marjorie's train, causing her to lurch wobbily as we began to leave the altar. And finally, a local woman I had once slept with stared at me from her aisle seat (she had sat on the bride's side, too) as we walked out, pursing her lips and working her jaw in an effort to communicate disgust for me and probably pity for Marjorie. I had noticed her earlier, and for a moment had been stricken with the notion that she was going to speak up when Dr. Johnson asked if anyone knew why Marjorie and I should not be joined together.

Thank God, she was sober and said nothing, and I forgot her as we walked down the aisle nodding at our friends. We passed into the light at the end of the tunnel and the thing was done.

I guess there must have been four or five hundred people at the club, a good two gin-and-tonics' worth of duty in the receiving line.

"You remember the Cranbrookes, darling, from Wilmington. 'Member he took you through United Bearings when you were a little boy?"

"Certainly. Mr. Cranbrooke. Mrs. Cranbrooke. Lovely thing you gave us."

"Why you're nice to remember, Mark," said Cranbrooke *père*, who had no more idea what his wife had sent us than I had. "Good luck, son, she's a real *dazz*ler . . ."

"And Horst Fitzpatrick? . . ."

"Hey, Horst, good t'see you."

"Real spellbinder, Mark. Jesus, beautiful, beautiful."

"Horst Fitzpatrick, lover."

" —— so much about you, Horst." Marjorie was at her most demure, offering her cheek to them. Horst, Hays, Dane Culliver, Wells, Tony, Alan, Eddy Grisling . . .

They were mainly Wilmingtonians — friends, and the sons and daughters of friends of my mother's from the old days. The older ones seemed concerned to reassure my mother about Routledge: "And it's *not* commutable — why Sandra, how wonderful! And those marvelous pin oaks! What a darling town! How wise you were to have moved here. How wise you were, darling! And she's lovely, just lovely."

Gush, all of it. It wasn't that they weren't fond of my mother and the son they remembered only as he had been at six or seven. I'm sure they were. But everything they said was so fatuous, and they said it with such practiced unctuosity, that the effect was cloying, saccharine.

Marjorie's people were there also, a smaller, more heterogeneous delegation, diminished by the claims of another wedding closer to home. This retinue comprised some eight principals, not including the maids of honor, and perhaps twenty horseholders. You will have heard of none of them, I think, except possibly Marjorie's congressman, once a roommate of her father's at Virginia, the moderate Republican Karl Feiling.

It was diverting to watch the two packs sniff one another, and even more amusing to watch the Routledgians sniff the less "social" among their own townspeople, whom my mother — a Tory democrat if there ever was one — had thoughtfully added to the guest list. She saw to their commingling, too:

"Harriet, darling, look who's *here!*"

"Yes?"

"You know Mr. Ferrazani, who works in the abattoir in New Haven? I'm going to whisk you two over to the bar for some champagne and nice bright conversation. *Mis*-ter Ferrazini, Miss Wilson."

"How ya' doin, honey?"

"That's it, that's right, get her a nice glass of champagne . . ."

My mother performed such offices many times that day. There was no harm in it, and she seemed not to notice that these fresh acquaintances usually didn't last more than five or ten minutes. Meantime the liquor was beginning to do its work among the gentry; a standard conversational lubricity now prevailed; there was much interpenetration of swaggering males and many idle invitations were exchanged.

From under the marquee came the tentative bleatings of a society orchestra. I took Marjorie by the arm and we moved over that part of the grounds the club hopefully had designated "the sward," towards the empty dance floor.

First Mr. Mark Davis and his good-natured band gave us "Everything's Comin' Up Roses," in the middle of which we were separated by her tough little linebacker of a father, who spun Marjorie away in a precarious series of concentric whorls in the general direction of the far end of the marquee, from which he could watch the finals of the club clay-court championships for a minute or two. I danced, or was rather led by my mother in a frenetic set of fox-trots which included "Mountain Greenery" and "It's De-lovely" and "So in Love," all the old songs rendered in that reedy *patois* for which Mr. Davis is known everywhere.

But Marjorie and I were handed back to each other at the opening bar of our song, "If Ever I Would Leave You," from *Camelot*, vulgarly believed to be one of the favorite ballads of the late young president: "Your hair with a lustarrr/that puts gold to shaymme." As I say, the Davis ensemble made little distinction as to beat or speed among the things they felt they should play, so that even "If Ever I Would Leave You" might as well have been "Black Bottom."

Just before the music stopped Marjorie bit me on the earlobe, causing some handclapping and a shriek or two. We twirled and pumped and kicked out our heels in that little fillip you do, pushed each other back a ways, keeping our fingers joined, so as to study each other and make certain that everyone else could see us studying each other, and factor what they saw into their fluttering visions of us making love that night, late, in Montego Bay. Perhaps they saw us, in John Fowles's wonderful phrase, "celebrating our orgasm" — *homo superior,* I should have thought — while fragrant Caribbean zephyrs stirred the curtains at the door to our balcony.

Our epithalamion continued. A swarthy fiddler caught us resting at our parents' table and serenaded us with the song from *Moulin Rouge*. Several of my friends from college who had been in a singing group called The Decibels offered a wry "Love for Sale," prompting my father-in-law to say he would have to speak to their leader, Mr. Goheen.

"Want to buy my wares?" Marjorie asked. We got up to dance again. I loved the fragrance of her hair and told her so and she told me it was a perfume created to suggest "nice" sex. I loved the way she felt next to me. Each time we would come back together from one of those little pushouts I would pull her very tight against me for the way her breasts felt under that merry widow contraption they wear under their wedding gowns; and we would twirl and pump some more, moving away from the stylish double-cutters buzzing around us. I remember with a clarity almost surreal the ardent, no-more-monkey-business, deep and so-in-love looks she was giving me. The fun had drained from her face.

Upstairs in the club about ten of us were crammed inside the golf-pro's bedroom. I was changing out of my cutaway and my ushers were doing what they felt the occasion demanded: Ferdy Smith, up from Quantico with a kind of Mohawk haircut, had poured champagne into a shoe and sloshed it over my head. Another cut-up had filled a Rameses prophylactic with Jergen's Lotion, knotted the thing and secreted it in my suitcase. "The fit'll hit the shan when she finds this!" he sniggered, prompting an erudite reflection by my best man on the banality of evil. (Marjorie later found the rubber and said, "What's in it — Jergen's Lotion?") Tad Crump and Paul Bergtold, meantime, having squirted shaving cream all over the getaway vehicle, a borrowed DB-4, were presenting me a splendidly bound volume titled "All I Know about Sex, by Mark Adams," full, of course, of empty pages. Meantime I felt safe from the heavier pranks. They couldn't very well get at the hotel room in Jamaica, and poor Crump's own genitals had been doused with printer's ink and Ben-Gay at his bachelor party two summers ago. I didn't think they'd try that. But what followed was a good deal worse.

A voice outside, my father-in-law's: "Mark, may I see you for a moment?"

I excused myself, grateful for the respite and expecting him to give me a check. "How you making it, sir?" I asked him. He was a powerful man, very short and compact. He tried to disguise the fact that he had almost no neck by having his barber trim his hair very high on the back of his head.

He saw me come out into the hall and began moving towards the central staircase end, away from the golf-pro's bedroom. At the same time, still without looking at me, he made a kind of "c'mere, buddy" gesture with his right hand. He wanted a little more privacy.

From the beginning our relationship had been an uneasy one, no different from the relationships of most prospective bridegrooms and fathers-in-law. He could still unblinkingly refer to his daughter as "my little girl," and to this day he calls her "princess" — second syllable accented — to her face.

"How you doing?" I repeated.

Well, he was doing just fine, just fine. Everything had been first-class. The people had been goddamned nice, hadn't they? He thought maybe they'd be a bunch of stuffed shirts, but they weren't. Came to scorn, stayed to praise. Mr. Semple was the solid paterfamilias, a burgher of Wall Street, very direct, very precise, usually angry. In college he had been a linebacker; but looking him over you would probably have taken him for a former marine drill instructor. Walking behind him I was noticing the vestiges of a severe childhood acne at the base of his neck, a condition that now made him look as though he'd caught some spent buckshot and hadn't bothered to dig it out. He must have been a tough diplomat.

At last he stopped. He leaned against the water cooler at the end of the hall and folded his hands together.

"Here, Mark," he said, reaching into his breast pocket. "Here's a check for five thousand dollars."

"Thank you, Paul. That's terribly generous of you. Really." Indeed it was exactly five times what I expected.

I had never addressed Mr. Semple by his Christian name before, and I thought I saw him start at the sound of it. Perhaps it was a liberty. Meantime he had leaned over the water cooler and drunk, and wiped his mouth on the back of his sleeve.

"Don't call me Paul and don't be quick to reach for the check. Never be quick to reach for a check, any kind of check."

There was a bare hint of levity in this. I had once paid a restaurant bill for us, and it had left me broke for a week.

"Sir?"

"I want to ask you a question, young man."

"Shoot. Anything." Looking back on it, I think I knew what he was going to ask from the tone of his question.

"You ever slept with my daughter?"

Had I ever slept with his daughter. That routine. "Come on, Mr. Semple."

"No. Not 'come on, Mr. Semple.' Have you ever *slept* with my daughter?"

I hadn't answered him fast enough, and I had not said the right thing. If I had replied in an outraged negative I imagine Mr. Semple would have embraced me like a mafioso greeting a lieutenant after a long prison spell. A vision of an enduring bonhomie and fine palship appeared briefly before me: hunting trips and good sippin' whiskey and talk of automotives and Commies . . .

He telegraphed nothing. His punch was thrown, or rather thrust at me with the force and velocity of a jackhammer, sighted and aimed along a line from his right shoulder to my face, aimed for the roots of my front teeth. It did not miss by much, either, the center knuckle striking an inch to the right of my nose and the rest of the fist catching me in the hollow of my cheek.

That was all there was to it. I never lost consciousness, but the force of the blow knocked my head back against a trophy case, or rather its frame, and I recall sliding down against it and into a kind of spread-eagled position on either side of his feet. I saw my shirtfront going scarlet as blood dripped on it, little bright pools expanding and merging together. I thought of that oil-slick counter-guerrilla tactic the French had in Vietnam and was amazed at how scarlet the blood was. It came burbling out lumpily as if the air were clotting it.

It did not appear he was going to kick me. I noticed his head shook with a faint palsy and I smirked at him.

"I'm going to give this check to your son, if you have a son, the day he's born. You conceited son-of-a-bitch, you'll name him after yourself. I'll only have to write 'junior' on it, after your name. Anything you want to say?"

I was completely lucid and considered the alternatives: "Fuck you" would be most satisfying, but — considering where he was standing — riskiest. There was also "Thanks, sir, I needed that." I decided on a middle course.

"These things happen. Some girls get pregnant before they get married."

"Happen, shit."

"They happen. You weren't any cherry when you got married."

"It happens I was, Adams. And we're talking about my daughter."

"My wife."

"You snotty little bastard." The next blow, this one openhanded, caught me up 'longside the head, as they say in the Carolinas. It was compact and well executed and it stung a great deal.

But this was the end of the violence. Mr. Semple now turned abruptly and walked back down the hall and I heard him take the back stairs two at a time. His *envoi* was characteristic: "Clean yourself up. Put on another one of those little fairy pink shirts and get your miserable ass outta here."

No one knows the truth of this story but Marjorie's father and me. I fobbed off the ushers with a tale about an angry rival who'd driven up from Far Hills. I told Marjorie what happened when we were on the plane.

"Did you hit him back? Did you defend yourself, darling?"

"I'm not about to hit your father, darling, not under any conditions. What I did was to take him by the wrists after the first little flurry, but he slipped one by me. But no, I wouldn't hit him."

"Thank God," she said.

The issue has never come up again. Neither Mr. Semple nor I bore a grudge against each other. I now call him Paul, have twice hit him up for money, and have the pleasure of saying that when I served in Vietnam he wrote me more than anyone except his little girl. He may not have liked young men getting to his daughter, but he hated Communism worse.

When we go to stay with the Semples he chases the women out of the living room on Sunday afternoons and we watch pro football together.

18

Marjorie miscarried in my mother's car on the way back from the airport after our honeymoon. If she had had a warning, she never told me about it.

She took it with her usual calm. The doctor told us it meant nothing for the future. It happened lots of times on the first go-round. I told Marjorie what a drunk at our wedding had told me: that she was the most *fecund* woman he had ever seen, and that she made him think of loins and begetting. A pleasant thing to say, I told him. "True, too," he said.

I want to remember Marjorie always as she was in Montego Bay. Very early in the mornings I would leave her and go down to the cool deserted beach to read. An hour later she would come to sit by me with her knees at her chin and her fingers trolling in the sand, saying nothing for a minute perhaps, and then, shyly, as if she were meeting me for the first time, "Hi, scholar." I remember her as she walked up through the shallow surf towards me at midday, the swaying weight and substance of her hips as she put one foot slowly and directly in front of the other as a child might walk on a sidewalk, trying to avoid the cracks; and, later, in the pinkish silvery haze of dusk, how she would reach down into the water for shells while she looked away at the sea.

I loved the down at her thighs; and at night, as she lay beside me on the great coverless bed, the chaste pallor of her hips bordered sharply by the mahogany of her thighs and waist. Our honeymoon was an idyll I had not really expected. All self-consciousness had vanished, and the complete happiness of our future together seemed assured.

Now she had miscarried and the reason for our having married must, for anyone but ourselves, have seemed to vanish. In the eyes of my friends I was worse than cuckolded. I could imagine their malicious glee — had I been one of them I would have shared it, I suppose — but now — well, they could go screw themselves.

In any case her recovery was very rapid. Late in October it was time, as Marjorie put it, for me to "play soldier." I had gone through the motions of ROTC at Princeton hoping for duty in France or Germany, thinking the odds overwhelmingly in favor of such an assignment. I had fluent French and German; and, gulled by the vague promises of some of the officers that these skills would certainly be utilized, I had asked for duty in Paris at the Embassy.

Instead I was ordered to a military establishment called Fort Hall: Fort Robert A. Hall, in Shermanville, South Dakota, "the biggest little city in the eastern Dakota." The post was named for a colonel prominent in the Indian fighting of the 1880's.

Calling itself the Home of the Western Infantry, Fort Hall consisted of a congeries of military schools and units: an understrength mechanized division, a chaplaincy school, an "institute" of mine warfare, and a famous noncommissioned officers' academy which cherished the motto "We Kill That Free Men May Live."

It is not a hard place to get to. If you are driving from the East you should plan on two nights in motels, five hundred miles motoring for almost three days. A fast spin over the Missouri near Council Bluffs and another hour's drive will bring you to Shermanville (pop. 27,654), whose main thoroughfare, Screaming Victory Drive, will lead you right to the main gate of Fort Hall. There a starchy MP will give you a finely detailed map of the Post, a guidebook and directions (whether you ask for them or not) to the Indian Fighter Museum. That is the Post's main attraction for the tourist.

Marjorie's reactions to the place were a mixture of shock, rooted in her naïveté about military matters, and quiet scorn. Instinctively she rebelled against the rituals of army life, especially its "social" activities, which struck her as false and labored; yet she found it hard to believe that the soldierly things she watched — enterprises that seemed mindless — were *intended* for some useless purpose. Surely there was a Grand Manipulator somewhere, "a general or something," she said, somebody who knew what he was doing and was doing it for intelligible and necessary reasons.

For example: several minutes after our arrival I went to get a physical, leaving her parked in a large macadam lot with the suggestion that she study a heavy green tome mailed to her after our wedding called *The Modern Army Wife*.

When I got back to the car, wilted by the fearsome heat and depressed by everything I had seen and heard, Marjorie told me the following strange tale. Let me say there was nothing *farouche* in her telling of the story, and that she seemed as mystified as a child while she related it.

For ten minutes, she said, nothing had happened. She had got well into the chapter on *The Lieutenant's Bride — Leader or Follower?* — the message of which (cunningly concealed but unmistakable) was that she had better really watch her step in This Wife's Army — when suddenly a screen door at the end of a barracks next to the parking lot had swung open, kicked by a sweating hairless man in fatigue clothes and boots. The man was very young and seemed miserable. He was hanging from a pipe which was suspended from the ceiling of the passageway leading to the door.

The door slammed shut, was kicked open again, and the young man now vaulted from the pipe to the ground outside. He ran at once to the blacktop.

Forty or fifty others followed him out, repeating the pipe-door-ground vault, and joined the first soldier in a kind of open square formation. Here they all made fists, clapped their fists to their chests, and began running in place. At the same time they set up a low unhappy moan: arrrhhhhhhh. They kept this up for several minutes.

Now there appeared another military man, this one obviously in authority and beside himself with rage. "Sound off like you got a pair!" he shouted. The low mournful hum of the soldiers was at once transmuted to a vicious growling. Meantime their faces reddened as they ran harder in place. Sweat poured from them and from time to time they slapped at the flies and mosquitoes swarming around their heads.

"Y'all let that little lady in the kyar hear ya sound off!" the sergeant screamed.

One of the soldiers was too zealous in his effort to please: he grinned and waved at Marjorie. But this only restimulated the sergeant's anger.

"You don't wave at no officer's wife in ranks. Drop down and gimme fifty!"

"Which arm, Sergeant?" they shouted back together. That was, I discovered later, the standard response to this order.

"Two arms for fifty!" the sergeant answered. He glanced over at Marjorie and nodded at her.

The soldiers struggled through their push-ups under the bleaching midday sun; and finally, his fury at last assuaged, the leader ordered them to their feet and marched them off.

There weren't any soldiers in Far Hills or at Wellesley. The only military men Marjorie had ever seen had been marines at the Embassy in London, and that had been many years ago. She told her little story quite deadpan — though, as she went along, I saw she understood what was being done. Later I found out that the pipe routine was prompted by the young soldiers' unwillingness to soil the floor of their hallway (scrubbed the night before with toothbrushes) and that the growling and running were considered by the authorities to be a means of inculcating *esprit* and a tough mental attitude.

Outwardly Marjorie was usually a very tolerant woman. This was fortunate for us both during those two years at the Home of the Western Infantry. Owing to my very junior rank we were assigned quarters in Porkchop Clusters (the name commemorating some forgotten success by American arms during the Korean War), a grim little collection of prefabricated Cape Cod houses dating from 1942, and built of sheet aluminum.

We need have no worries about termites, was one of our consolations — as a sergeant told me, "The fuckers cain't chew alu-minium, Lootenant." There was also the advantage that we were only three blocks from the commissary to consider. And that we had a pine tree in our front yard. And that we were close enough to the main road that the spray trucks could spray our house each summer night with insect repellent, an hygienic if noisome business. (Marjorie to spray-truck driver: "I don't like this, you know." Sergeant, drolly: "You'll learn to like it, ma'am.") Finally, getting back to the metal house — a frolicsome old NCO from Post Engineers told us that if we lost our house key, we could always let ourselves in with a can opener.

The interior walls of our dwelling were painted sage gray, it being forbidden, further, to "decorate or abuse" them. If we wanted to hang pictures we would attach the sons-of-bitches by means of screws wound into pre-

existing holes. The henna-colored linoleum floors, meantime, should for best value be kept in a high state of
police.

Alas, we had few sons-of-bitches to screw in: two
Dürer prints and Marjorie's graduation certificate from
Wellesley. We covered the floors with worn carpets the
quartermaster gave us; the same agency also provided
beds and tables, since our own furniture was — they
imagined — tied up at a railhead in Chicago . . .

As I say, a trying time for Marjorie and me, though
not without its measure of humor: the sexual congress of
basset hounds during a military ceremony for a visiting
brigadier called George Lemming; the incredible disap-
pearance of a 105 Howitzer from the gun park — the
weapon remained missing for almost eleven weeks; the
appearance of my first sergeant at a formal company
dinner in a short-sleeved *suit*. Things like that. I had
convinced myself that I would be entertained by the
Army; annoyed perhaps, but never shocked or outraged.
Meredith tells us that "when one has attained that felicitous point of wisdom from which one sees all mankind
to be fools, the diminutive objects may make what new
moves they please, one does not marvel at them: their
sedateness is as comical as their frolic, and their frenzies
more comical still." It was useful at Fort Hall always to
strive for this felicitous point; for me certainly, and for
Marjorie even more.

We were summoned our second night to the home of
Colonel Garret Fairbrooke, commanding officer of the
training brigade to which I was assigned as motor-pool

officer. The colonel lived in a large stucco house up on Spear's Bluff, an appropriately named eminence for a man of his quality. That he was a "highly military individual" was the conventional wisdom of the Post. He was said to be absorbed in appearances: shiny things elicited his happy approval; tarnished objects his rage. An erect carriage in his view proclaimed devotion to duty; a slumping or portly young warrior could not be expected adequately to perform his tasks. An officer whose hands were occupied in stroking a swagger stick was alert, commendably importunate; an officer whose hands reposed in his pockets was lazy and permissive. A tidy barracks promised efficiency of action; a barracks in which foot lockers were unaligned (for example) was a lamentably apt index of defective teamwork, promising systemic dissolution in the crucible of combat.

Fairbrooke met us at the door, immaculate in a white linen suit. He had the glabrous, arresting appearance of a human mutant of the third millennium, A.D. All the hair had been shaved from his head, and his high forehead bulged at either side, as though his skull had too many brains for its size. His face had the sallow-orange coloring of a military bureaucrat who spent half his waking hours under the florescent lights of army offices, the rest driving around in jeeps. In physique he was slender and leathery, fleet-looking.

"Lieutenant and Mrs. Adams, I see!"

"Good evening, colonel. My wife Marjorie."

"How do you do?" He stood back and took her in. "You did very well, young man. Recently married?"

"Just a month ago, sir."

"The old ring in the nose, ay?"

"Afraid so, sir."

"In my day second lieutenants did not often marry. Will you come this way?"

We crossed the foyer to a closet under the stairwell, noticing three or four other newly arrived lieutenants and their wives had preceded us. They all sat in the living room, solemnly nodding at a woman I took to be Mrs. Fairbrooke.

The colonel fixed us drinks in glasses bearing the West Point crest and we went in to join the others. But let me say here that the colonel's living room was dominated by a painting so utterly unexpected that it caused Marjorie to gasp — I mean, literally — and that this painting was nothing less than a laminated representation of Jesus Christ.

It was no small portrait. I should guess it measured some three by five feet, and it showed a quite stern Jesus, a hard-nosed ascetic in a heavy gown of gray samite. He was lean and sunburned like his owner, and like him seemed inclined to be suspicious: for he had flip-flop eyes that followed you wherever you went in the room.

Philistinism I had expected, but this was too much. I was more depressed than amused. I was going to have to work under Colonel Fairbrooke, perhaps directly under him (I doubted he would leave me in the motor pool for two years). I now imagined we wouldn't have much to talk about besides business.

But he surprised me. He must have been used to people's reactions when they saw the picture, because he had what sounded like a ready explanation: "Don't blame me, Adams," he said. "I'm as active an Anglican as you'll find west of the Missouri, except maybe for

Bishop Pike. No, that's my good wife's picture. Doris, the Adamses."

"How do you do?" said the dull woman. "I am a Georgia Baptist, and I see nothing wrong in having a picture of Jesus in the parlor. Garret has a picture of Frederick the Great in his study."

Good point, I told her. And Marjorie, who had made a neat recovery, was warm and polite to Mrs. Fairbrooke — to whom, in some yet undisclosed way, she would be socially answerable. "It *is* a good likeness, colonel," I said. "The artist has captured a side to Him I hadn't thought about before. The Lord Mighty in Battle, the Messiah foreseen in the Old Testament histories. Perhaps the picture's quite appropriate here in your house."

But he neither laughed nor made any follow-up remarks — say, something about the Book of Joshua or Oliver Cromwell. He took us around the room to meet the other young officers and their wives, making quick little speeches about all of the men in which he typecast them by stating the names of the colleges from which they had graduated and their assignments in the Brigade. Three of the four lieutenants had recently left the Mil'try Academy; the other was a Rot-see man, "like you, Adams."

Like me, except that he had gone to Prairie View A & M, and was black. He was also easily the most relaxed of that taut little circle of military people. He threw me a wonderful smile as we shook hands, and the message his eyes conveyed was unmistakable: "What bullshit is this?"

We got down grimly to the business at hand, our formal housecall. It was soon apparent that we had settled into a nest of silly post-adolescents, not counting the black lieutenant and Fairbrooke — the latter deployed a certain compelling panache. The three officers from the Mil'try Academy talked like men in their fifties. They were so overawed by the military station of their host, who so palpably (it seemed to them) bore on his shoulders the awful burden of the defense of the Republic, that they nodded abruptly in assent to each of his declarations. They sat on the edges of their chairs, leaning forward in rapt concentration, their hands folded together and hanging stiffly between their knees. The colonel would hammer home certain points with gestures that reminded me of President Kennedy's — like a man throwing darts — and with each statement and each thrust of the finger the lieutenants would recoil backwards like artillery pieces.

They had little to say themselves, and they dared not discuss anything outside the general subject of national defense and the specific topic of the Brigade:

"My people's rifles are pitted. Pitted before they got 'em."

"Mine're pitted too. Where'd they get these firesticks from, colonel."

Fairbrooke smiled indulgently at the salty archaism. "The line units have the good weapons, Lieutenant Frost. The training depots the bad. I doubt anyone'll invade us here. Certainly not the Canadians."

One lieutenant, who had earlier asked the colonel to make him his favorite drink, a Brandy Alexander, solicited the colonel's views on the worsening situation in Vietnam. It was only a month or two after the Gulf of Tonkin incident.

Lieutenant Frost, certain Fairbrooke would allow a discourtesy because of the correctness of his views, answered the question: "You let those people horse around with you, you're asking for it."

Mrs. Fairbrooke solemnly nodded agreement.

"What's your view, Adams?" the colonel asked me.

"I quite agree, sir." In those days I certainly did.

"I don't agree," said Marjorie. She could not have evoked a more stunned silence if she had farted. "I don't see the point."

Now saying what Marjorie said to a party of military people in 1964 was something like calling the Goldwater-Miller ticket "pinko." The remark was even more surprising coming from a second lieutenant's wife; and the other women, plump and creamy-complected under lacquered beehives, exchanged sharp and knowing looks. One of them made that ghastly *tch* sound with her tongue.

"You don't see the point, my dear?" Fairbrooke inquired. He for one was unruffled, or appeared to be, and he put the question gently. "Do you *know* what these people are capable of? Do you know they're bent on invading a country to which we have treaty commitments?"

"Countries can ignore treaties when it's not in their interest to honor them," Marjorie replied. "I don't see the point of any wars, really. They create more problems than they solve. They get out of control as soon as they're started anyway." She looked around at the others, curious about their reactions but somehow conveying the impression she didn't care whether they disagreed with her or not.

"Are you a pacifist, Mrs. Adams?" Lieutenant Frost demanded.

"What do you mean when you say 'pacifism,' lieutenant?"

"Well, you know, like all killing is wrong no matter what."

"Well, I don't like killing, and it usually isn't necessary. You don't like killing, do you, Mr. Fairbrooke?"

"Colonel, darling," I reminded her.

"Colonel." She gave him her most demure and enchanting smile.

Colonel Fairbrooke did not answer Marjorie. Instead he asked her to excuse herself and join him in the kitchen. They would have a "little talk." Marjorie followed him out, and after a respectful interval the conversation resumed.

"Quite a little spitfire," said Lieutenant Frost.

I looked at him and did not comment.

"She ever been around the Army before?"

"No, not really."

"Well, she'll learn."

I felt great loathing for him, almost enough to make me want to put my hands around his neck. But the black officer answered him before I could say or do anything I'd probably regret afterwards.

"What'll she learn, Frost?"

"Oh, you know."

"No, I don't know. Learn to agree with you? Learn to be nervous and uptight and careful around right-wingers like yourself? Learn to keep her mouth shut because she's a woman? A lieutenant's wife? What the hell's the matter with you? You think this is the German General Staff?"

Frost said nothing. Like most military people he was

lousy at comebacks, at bon mots. He looked at the others, and I sensed he was trying to communicate that it would be unseemly of him to argue with a black lieutenant.

"Perhaps Garret's telling her what to learn in the kitchen," said Mrs. Fairbrooke. She said it with a sympathetic smile for me and the black, and the tension subsided quickly. The matter was the colonel's responsibility.

Marjorie and Fairbrooke returned at that moment.

"Well, I think we understand each other now," he announced. He clapped his hands and rubbed them together, the officious gimmick of all Men in Charge who want to end embarrassing silences. The conversation ran into unconnected runnels: the army football team's prospects, the Post Vet, the softness of the recruits, the wild-eyed liberalism of the Ivy League, the benefits of owning naugahyde furniture if your profession required you to move often. After ten or fifteen minutes of this the colonel looked down at his watch, indicating our call should be concluded.

As for Marjorie — she was well into her second gaffe of the evening. She was asleep.

19

Yet we settled into army life more easily than I had feared. If the routine was intellectually debilitating, if the eastern Dakota was no grove of cultural activity, if the professionals were as tense and worried as Manhattan account executives — still, the life had its pleasures. One stayed very fit, the troops were fun to be around, and my books finally arrived. The violent evening squalls swirling off the prairie west of us were a marvelous music to go to sleep to, especially as played on our aluminum roof. And it transpired that Fairbrooke was a decent fellow after all. He did not leave me in the motor pool for long, but arranged for me to command a training platoon after my apprenticeship there was completed. ("I desire well-rounded people in my Brigade," he said. He always said "desire" when he meant "want.") He told me without sarcasm that he had admired Marjorie's forthrightness the other evening, even though her views were unacceptable to his philosophy of life.

So, while I roved through the rows of squat green jeeps and trucks on inspection (which I conducted by passing my little finger along the tops of the windshield wipers, where dust was said to settle overnight, and by kicking at the tires of the vee-hickals to assure their proper inflation), Marjorie had ample time to explore the world of army women: not those in uniform, but those married to the officers of the Brigade.

The Incidents of the Prayer and the Ashtray, and — I am afraid — the deep reservoirs of ill will which silently formed behind them, made a condign summary of her experience in that grim little world. Nor will it do to excuse her conduct in either affair on the grounds that she was again pregnant, as one of her friends tried to do later. Indeed Marjorie's behavior in both was perfectly in character, and I was delighted with it. Take the Ashtray incident first.

At one of the morning coffees the wives of the officers held each week, Mrs. Fairbrooke announced plans for a sherry party to be held in honor of Mrs. Manley R. Severn, wife of the Commanding General, Western Infantry Indoctrination Command. This lady, whom Mrs. Fairbrooke characterized as a "handsome and truly wonderful person" (the way, say, your roommate at college might tell you your blind date has a truly remarkable personality), had graciously accepted the Brigade wives' invitation to be its guest of honor. (Not to put too fine a point on it, she had disingenuously angled for the invitation, foreseeing she would be free during her husband's inspection visit to the Home of the Western Infantry.) Mrs. Fairbrooke further cautioned the wives that Mrs. Severn was known for her liverish temperament, and that she was as much a stickler for proprieties as her husband, a tough old bird who gloried in the nickname of Manley the Manhandler. Great attention must be paid to detail. A committee must be formed to prepare for the occasion.

Upon reflection Mrs. Fairbrooke decided that one committee would not do. Subcommittees were indicated: subcommittees for (1) invitations, (2) decorations and entertainments, (3) hors d'oeuvres and (4) "escort and general hospitality."

Marjorie was put in charge of the last of these committees: her husband was only a lieutenant but her father was a diplomat. She and the other committee chairwomen reported the following morning to Spear's Bluff for detailed instructions.

Marjorie remembers the conversation as going something like this:

Mrs. Fairbrooke: "Now, dear, how would you want to treat a general's lady?"

Marjorie: "I suppose the same way I'd treat a friend of my mother's. Courteously but not obsequiously. She's hardly the Duchess of Buccleuch."

F: "I see, dear. What do you mean when you say 'not obsequiously'?"

M: "Unfawning."

F: "Yes, you would just be polite with her, very good. You would want to make her comfortable in a group of women she had never met before."

M: "Certainly."

F: "Alright, then. You and I will meet Mrs. Severn at the door of the Corregidor Cubbyhole, at the club, and make her feel welcome. Make nice small talk with her, you know."

M: "Yes?"

F: "She would want to hear something of our projects here, the Red Cross and so on. Also she is interested in foliage."

M: "Interested in foliage."

F: "Yes. Then I'll get her a sherry, and then you take her around the room and introduce her to some of the wives. Oh, and yes, she's a fairly heavy smoker, so have Patsy or someone keep an ashtray with her."

M: "I'm not sure I understand."

F: "Well, we'll all be walking around, don't you know, and Mrs. Severn won't have any place to put her ash."

M: "Yes?"

F: "So appoint someone to walk around with her with an ashtray. That's only basic courtesy."

M (Entering admirably into the spirit of the plan):
"Is Mrs. Severn right- or left-handed?"

F: "Right-handed as I recollect. The last time we
served with them was in the Berlin Brigade in '58. Yes,
right-handed."

M: "So my appointee would take position off her right
side?"

F: "Yes, that will do very nicely. And she would want
to keep up with Mrs. Severn wherever she's circulating."

M: "Could she excuse herself after Mrs. Severn ex-
tinguishes her cigarette?"

F: "I don't think that would be too wise, dear. As I
said before, she's a heavy smoker."

Thus their conversation ended, and they and the other
chairwomen went to the kitchen for coffee and cookies.

The great day arrived. General Severn inspected the
Training Brigade, the recruits standing pale and shaky at
attention under a slate Dakota sky, resembling, it struck
me at the time, an assembly of terrified goslings. Severn
looked them over with a thoroughness that did not belie
his reputation, barking out short little questions about
the ranges of the weapons they presented for him to
inspect, occasionally making adjustments of their equipment. He was impressed with what he saw, and thoughtfully ordered that they be dismissed and excused from
barracks' inspection. I left the formation and went home
to Porkchop Clusters.

Meantime the sherry party had begun at the club.
With its affecting decor — a coordinated scheme of
turquoise and antique gold — its concealed speakers
yielding their gentle strains of Muzak, its henna floors
polished to a dazzling sheen, its deep naugahyde sofas

and settees, its imaginative decorations (the admirable industry of Committee #3 should be acknowledged), its silently efficient young waiters in spotless white duck, and its great center table with its sumptuous burden of hors d'oeuvre (in which, alas, "rabbit food" and dips predominated unduly) — with all these things, the Corregidor Cubbyhole now made a matchless refectory for the entertainment of the wife of a general officer.

The wives and other invitees from neighboring units had thoughtfully arrived twenty minutes early, clothed after the fashion prescribed for them in *The Modern Army Wife:* "hose," smart but not overstated hats, white gloves, stylish suits. They stood about in their little company cliques exchanging gossip like their counterparts in civil life: all of them, that is, but Mrs. Fairbrooke and her social assistants Marjorie and Mrs. Patsy Kariani. Theirs was the duty of welcoming Mrs. Severn; theirs the charge to make her as happy as the Training Brigade appeared to have made her husband. Let no one doubt the solemnity of their undertaking.

An old but beautifully maintained Chrysler purred under the porte-cochere at the main door to the Fort Hall Officers' Club, and Mrs. Severn was handed out by her husband's aide. She strode through the main ballroom with the welcoming committee to the Corregidor Cubbyhole. (Marjorie describes Mrs. Severn, incidentally, as a most cordial and attractive woman, elegantly clothed for the occasion in a Givenchy midi. She had neither hat nor gloves.)

They went into the Cubbyhole.

Patsy Kariani veritably brandished her ashtray, Marjorie said — a receptacle that looked like a crystal ball sawed in half — and asked Mrs. Severn if she would like to commence smoking right away. "No, my dear," the lady responded good-naturedly, "I just put one out." She moved at the head of their little phalanx, pressing into the coveys of chattering females like a politician going for the heart of a crowd.

Mrs. Kariani took her assignment with more seriousness, perhaps, than even Mrs. Fairbrooke had bargained for. Have you ever seen two spiffy military men walking together in a city? You know how, now and again, one of them will execute that little half-skip to get in step with the other? Mrs. Kariani now executed one of those little skips, crossing behind Mrs. Severn as a destroyer cuts across the wake of its flagship, getting in step and moving to the cigarette side of Mrs. Severn in the same economical motion. Again her arm came up with the ashtray, and again the inquiry was made. "Now will you smoke, Mrs. Severn?"

"Alright, darling." Mrs. Severn took a Gauloise out of her purse and fitted it into a tortoise-shell holder and lit it.

Mrs. Kariani waited patiently for the ash to form, hopping around and trying to keep station with her ashtray. It was of course a most unsatisfactory and embarrassing operation, and more trouble lay ahead. This was when Mrs. Severn, who by now had had enough of what she inferred was some insolent skullduggery, tried to stub out her second cigarette in the hand-held ashtray. Whether what followed was deliberate or not we cannot know, but she plunged the used cigarette into the ashtray with enough force to dislodge it from Mrs. Kariani's hand.

The ashtray landed on Mrs. Fairbrooke's large toe and broke it.

Good soldier that she was, Mrs. Fairbrooke admitted only to some localized pain and surprise. She managed to limp through the remainder of the "social," to see Mrs. Severn out to her car with a warm invitation that she come back as soon as Manley (greatly daring, this, referring to the general by his Christian name) was ordered by the authorities to inspect Fort Hall again. Thus ended the Ashtray incident.

In case you are wondering whether or not Marjorie should be held responsible for the "accident," I can tell you that she told me that night in bed that she *was* — at least to the extent of having magnified the seriousness of her appointment to Patsy Kariani. I do not think Marjorie wished to hurt Mrs. Fairbrooke in any physical way; probably she wanted only to point up the folly of the Ashtray order. But she did laugh at the result, and I can tell you that the order has never been promulgated since by Mrs. Fairbrooke, or, as far as I know, by any American military functionary's wife anywhere.

20

About a month after I got my orders to Vietnam, only three weeks after the birth of our second child, there occurred the incident of the Prayer.

Births and orders to war are milestones in a marriage I suppose, and in our case the birth of our son and the arrival of the expected orders came in the very dead of a howling gray winter, a winter which, because it so far surpassed in length and intensity the winter we had prepared ourselves to endure, had the effect of palpable, physical oppression. The thin metal roof of our house sagged under its thick burden of snow; the frigid Dakota winds whipped and curdled each snowstorm with such violence that it became impossible to keep the house temperature much above 60°. One night I had a vision of the oil heater exploding in hungry spits of flame, a scalding wildfire which, since it could not burn the aluminum, began to melt it. The ridiculous house fell away dripping into slag, burning and melting us with it, and that spring we were wrought into a statue of an Indian war general.

To this time we had jogged along happily enough. We were acquiring children and cats and books, and Marjorie had absorbed herself in them all, projecting a grim private contentment which slowly began to annoy me. I despised the Army, of course, as she did. I can say only that prolonged involvement in its inanities, its drab make-work projects, with its coarse professionals and their uptight wives, did bring with it a certain dulling of our own sensibilities; and that this kept me on an even keel at work and socially. It was as though each morning before we woke up we were given huge shots of procaine.

I remembered Marjorie's first words to me. "Lucretius, do you read *that?*" I had read him once in the Dryden translation and I remembered the lines at the beginning of his poem: "What hath this bugbear death to frighten man/If souls can die as well as bodies can?" I felt it no exaggeration to think we were both somehow dead of spirit: dead in the absence of our friends, of the things we loved, in our enforced absorption in the mad dulling social activities of . . . We had been spoiled,

Marjorie's father said to her one night on the phone. Why, his generation had had to give up everything for the sake of defending their country; Mark's father had given his life, etcetera. As I say, however, the situation that had brought on my self-pity entailed its own anodyne. Nothing really bothered us except the superficial irritants of weather and the remoteness of Fort Hall and army life. But these were enough.

It was about this time, too, not much more than two years after our marriage in Routledge, that we stopped loving each other. Perhaps such things can never be dated exactly, except when one of the two people involved reveals himself in some sharp incident wholly undeserving of the other's respect. And in our case, thrown largely on each other's resources, forced together that winter at Fort Hall, the depletion of love came slowly and unremarked. I was conscious only that we were both somehow wandering, that while I was still comfortable with Marjorie, the old regenerative exhilaration of our sex had disappeared, and that slowly we were beginning to object to each other's values and habits.

If anything, Marjorie's so-called Prayer Incident should have arrested my growing alienation from her, because her role in it was very much of a piece with her performances at Tanglewood and in the art gallery in Hartford and its miserable aftermath and her announced pacifism, and these had been things which had made me love her more, had deepened her inscrutability and made her (since they made her seem more inaccessible) more desirable. But what the thing did, mainly, was to increase my exasperation with the Army. My laughter was becoming bitter where it had once been amused. I was growing contemptuous of those Fairbrooke called my brother officers and their wives, sickened by their caviling, beaten-down attitudes.

Now it happened that Mrs. Fairbrooke was an un-reconstructed lackey, a naturally subordinate person madly absorbed in her husband's grandiose schemes for restoring luster to his somewhat tarnished reputation. Fortunately these schemes rarely impinged on my own round of professional duties, but I was aware of them: after all, the successful colonels were all going off to our splendid little war; at the very least they were scurrying through the corridors of the Pentagon like hypertensive rodents, hoping for preferment and promotion, and above all, orders to command positions in Vietnam.

Fairbrooke feared for his lack of visibility. He decided to "host" a conference of senior officers in March, officers who would be lectured on counter-insurgency techniques by recognized experts for academia and the services. None of us lieutenants was involved in the conference except as go-fors and progress-swellers, but, as before, the wives of the Brigade were to help out with a luncheon for the wives of the conferees.

As far as I could make out, the other women didn't care for Marjorie. They felt she put on airs, that her silver and china and *things* represented a vulgar display for the wife of a junior officer. Her pacifism was well known, though she certainly never played it up, and they had an idea she was bored with them. In this they were right.

Only Mrs. Fairbrooke liked and cultivated Marjorie's friendship. "I a-dore your wife," she said to me one night over her Shirley Temple. "She's so sure of herself, so organized, she always knows what to do." For this reason Mrs. Fairbrooke sought her advice on all sorts of "occasions." It was enough that Marjorie always knew what to do, and that she was the daughter of a retired member of the diplomatic service. Mrs. Fairbrooke resolutely ignored the undercurrent of unapproving gossip about Marjorie.

As before, Marjorie was invited to Spear's Bluff to offer her suggestions as to how the luncheon could be made successful, with the difference that this time at least twelve other women were invited also. The trouble began almost immediately.

"I want a volunteer to say grace before the meal," said Mrs. Fairbrooke.

Marjorie objected at once: "I don't think you or anyone has any right to have grace said before lunch. You've got atheists in the audience . . . Catholics, Protestants, Jews, humanists. Grace is out of keeping in a situation like that."

The other women "froze like porcelain," as Marjorie told the story. Their shock soon changed to the outrage they imagined Mrs. Fairbrooke expected of them, however, and their outrage was transmuted to a sense of triumph that literally shone in their faces. They had seen their enemy challenge her only ally, wound and enrage her, desecrate her religion, and haughtily, imperturbably, dare to trample upon the icon of her faith.

Listening to Marjorie I was remembering a summer spent at ROTC Camp in Indiantown Gap, in particular a Sunday morning when several hundred of us cadets had had to endure an interminable harangue from a local minister in chapel — a harangue boiling over with jeremiads. "There are no fire escapes in Hell!" he shouted, no redemption from the awful flames to which we, by our swinish behavior, were assuring our condemnation. It seemed some of the cadets ("You know who you are!") had drunkenly taken on the daughter of a friend of the preacher, and he, like the stolid, hard-nosed colonel he no doubt wished himself to be, was berating the many for the sins of several. And suddenly an exasperated cadet from Richmond had lurched to his feet: "Certify you believe that swill," he screamed. "You're a dis-grace to your cloth, parson!" In the deathly pall that separated this outburst from the hobnailed clomping of the MPs coming to take the cadet away I looked at the prim faces all around me — faces at once frozen in shock and glee — faces that must have looked exactly like those of the Brigade ladies in Mrs. Fairbrooke's kitchen. Marjorie had challenged them collectively, had said the unsayable. They were too stunned to respond. But there was no one to take Marjorie away. Only sounds of the kitchen equipment punctuated the terrible silence. Finally, a minute or more having gone by, Mrs. Fairbrooke pushed back her chair and stood up, studying the faces of the other women, one by one, trying to gauge their reactions to Marjorie's blasphemy and rankest insubordination. The colonel's lady need not have worried, however. For, as she walked out of the kitchen, all the other ladies but Marjorie got up to follow her. In a few minutes Marjorie could hear them discussing plans for the luncheon once again, discussing them, moreover, under the stern uplifting gaze of the laminated Christ. A notably long grace was written that morning, by a committee of three women most scandalized by Marjorie's statement, and it was later pronounced with much relish by Mrs. Fairbrooke herself. The luncheon was a great success.

Marjorie has never exaggerated. I must ask you to remember, too, that several months had elapsed between the Ashtray and Prayer incidents. And if Marjorie's involvement with the other women of the Brigade had been uncomfortable, she had rarely commented on it. Thus the prayer business stood out in high relief. It released Marjorie from any further official association with her former ally; it cut off all our social obligations; and it brought about my last interview with Colonel Fairbrooke, whom I saw from time to time in my duties, but with whom I had had no serious talk in over a year.

He was in quite good spirits when I went into his office. The conference had passed off with good notices, and he had secured his coveted orders to command duty in Vietnam.

He had some advice for me, he said, and it was this:

I was a good young officer and I could make a productive and fulfilling career for myself in the Army. There was only one obstacle he could see, and he reckoned that with patience and energy on my part that obstacle could be removed from my path to military distinction.

I waited for him to criticize my flip attitude. Instead, looking up from his nails, which he had been grooming with a K-bar, he identified the obstacle as something I had probably not considered before: "Your wife, Adams."

He rose up magisterially and directed me to calm down. "She's a wonderful girl, we all know that. But Adams, life is compromise, give and take, and Marjorie's got to learn that fine art. Doris's told me about their little set-to. She's a big woman, it didn't bother her. It's woman-crap anyway. But the other women were hurt, you know, because they're young and they're still groping their way along. What Marjorie's got to do is use the old tact."

The old tact, he went on, that I was noted for. I hadn't given anyone any shit, he said; and coming from a man who did not swear often, his statement communicated that his wife had given him plenty of shit about Marjorie.

"Otherwise she'll get hurt, and you'll get hurt, just as if your son shot out all the windows in Post Elementary. So talk to her, guide her along, get her rolling with the currents a little more. You get home from Vietnam you'll find your advice has had plenty of time to sink in. OK?"

"Yes, sir."

"Good!" He clapped his hands and rubbed them together. "How're the kids?"

"Fine, sir."

"Good! You know, Adams, we think you and Marjorie are real special. You'll have a lot of fun in the Army, a *hell* of a lot of fun. Just get your old lady a little more tolerant."

I nodded at him.

"Go get 'em, tiger. Keep your head down over there. You're not tall like I am, but the gooks shoot low."

There it was, as simple as that: my problem boiled down to manageable dimensions, corrective action recommended with the assurance that it could not possibly fail, a hearty farewell from a man who knew less about Marjorie and me than he did about the U.S. Navy. Everything was simple to a man like Fairbrooke. All you had to do was see it his way.

21

"Go up and say goodbye to him, Mark."

It was the end — I should say the butt-end because it had been miserable — of our month's leave together in Routledge before I left for Vietnam. Though we were staying at my mother's, Marjorie had arranged to spend most of the year with her parents in Far Hills, and Mr. Semple in a great access of goodwill had hired a nurse for the children. This kind act led to several fights between us, I foolishly arguing that Marjorie would spend all her time in New York and ignore the children. I had said unforgivable things to her at the beginning of our leave and spent the last three weeks trying unsuccessfully to live them down.

I went upstairs to the guest room where my son lay in a bassinet. I remember the morning vividly. Outside the late winter wind had died quietly away, and the snow that had fallen the night before had settled to a terrible minatory whiteness. It is a morning defined in my memory by great unbordered mirrors, by the light cast undiffused to meet them through the windows of the living room and study of my mother's house, reflected sternly back to irradiate things unnoticed before: objects of silver and glass; clocks, highboys, chiffoniers and Parsons tables of burnished shining mahogany; walls of salmon and pink. I suddenly saw my mother's house as I had not seen it before. I saw the things she cherished in the purity of their archetypes: cold and perfect, wrought sparkling by the awful December sun, the treeless white lawn outside shining like a vacant winter beach.

The passing of time registered only in the split-crack-puff of icicles dropping from the eaves. I was in my son's room, staring down at his tiny warmth and pinkness, willing that he should know I loved him, that he was my child as well as Marjorie's, that whatever father might be provided for him if I were killed would not be of his flesh as I was. He lay covered to his neck on his chest and knees, one arm exposed above the saffron coverlet palm upwards. I put my forefinger in his palm and left it there unclutched.

"He's a dear little thing, darling." It was not Marjorie, but my mother. "Isn't he *cunning?*"

We left the house and my mother drove us down long black corridors hewn out of the snow. At the airport we had a drink and watched my plane taxi in close under the window of the lounge. I said goodbye to my mother here, and to Marjorie at the gate, where, sick with self-hate and anguish, trying in a moment to redeem what I had been to her in the last two years of our marriage, I could only say to her, "Darling."

"I know," she said. She squeezed my hand as though I were a schoolboy dropping her off after a prom, kissed my cheek and ran back upstairs. I saw her drinking with my mother from the plane, and they did not see me wave at them.

22

"You got a letter from your wife, captain. You got time to read it now or you want me to leave it with your things?"

I told the sergeant I'd take it with me. We were going up in the C & C ship to look over the new AO — the area of operations into which our battalion had been inserted two nights before. If Colonel Hanks didn't come along I could read it in the chopper.

We had set up a small field headquarters in a tiny clearing not far from the base of a steaming hump of a hill in the highlands. Wenlock Edge, I wanted to name it on the map overlays, but Hanks would have none of that. Two of the companies had already gone out; the third remained to provide security for the headquarters and the 105 battery which lay just inside its perimeter. By now the clearing had been somewhat enlarged, battered and scraped out of the jungle, so that the hueys could get in two at a time — the Command and Control ship, medivacs (none of which, blessedly, had yet been needed) and resupply choppers, bobbing down from the sky like tadpoles suspended in swamp water, nosing in gingerly, flicking their tails back and forth while they looked for places to burrow, rustling and stirring the underside of the jungle canopy as they dropped down on us.

I got aboard with the executive officer and the S-2. "Where's the Old Man?"

"He's staying."

"He's beat, Adams," the S-2 said, and then he hollered out the door in the direction of a stack of C-ration crates and 105 boxes, "Don't commit the Reserve, colonel," a lame private joke. Hanks was accustomed to yell the same thing from the chopper when he went up with the whole command group, leaving only a buck sergeant to man the radios and coordinate things from the ground: "Don't commit the Reserve, Sergeant Fischer!" And Fischer, the callow, epicene youth who had given me Marjorie's letter, would show a lazy half-arm in acknowledgement, his face set in its usual asinine grin. There never was any reserve to speak of and Fischer had never commanded anything larger than a corporal's guard at Fort Dix. But he was a real operator.

I laughed at the S-2, and he yelled the same thing again, and this time, as the rotor finally sucked us off the ground, I saw an arm go up straight, a puppet-like motion, and I saw that the supine figure with its head propped against one of the cases of C-rations was Colonel Hanks, and that he had heard the S-2. Ordinarily Hanks would have ordered the chopper back down and given us a good prickly working-over: "That shit don't get it, fella, not when there's troops around," and all our careful cultivation of Hanks's friendship would come to nothing. He liked to distance himself from his people, even from the older members of his personal staff, and you could never get too close to him. "He's a hard," the sergeant major would say. "Ain't nobody ever got near him." But we admired Hanks; we tried to loosen him up, and we would keep trying for the rest of our time with him.

Now he was too tired and we were suddenly too far

away. The C & C was an H-model huey, immensely powerful. We were even with the jungle canopy, and then above it; the helicopter abruptly stopped climbing and shot forward, practically skimming the jade fronds of the canopy, and headed away down the ridgeline towards the open valley we wanted to look over.

Major Remick sat at the open door to my right with a submachine gun in his lap. He wore wrap-around sun glasses that allowed him to look where he wanted without your knowing what he was looking at, and he was chewing gum with his mouth open. As always he wore an expression both insolent and amused, and as always I was seeing him in pinstripes and a snap-brim hat, riding on the running board of an old Chevy looking for people to shoot. He called the colonel "boss"; junior officers were invariably "clown." "Commere, clown." I admired him.

There's always been someone like Remick in my life. Horst Fitzpatrick, whom you met briefly at my wedding, was nine or ten when I was seven, and he used to sit in our pew with us in church and ape the motions of the communicants at the railing by making a fist and jerking his head back like Randolph Scott tossing off a shot of whiskey in a bar room. At those times he would look over at me and calmly assess the havoc he had caused: I would be on the verge of wetting my pants and just at the point where I could no longer hold back my laughter, and finally it would gather at the back of the roof of my mouth and come bursting out my nose. I would be in agony for the rest of the service, and Fitzpatrick would come up to my mother afterwards and tell her to take it easy on me when we got home. "He's just a little kid, Mrs. Adams." My mother thought him a "well-set-up" young man. "You never see Horst rollicking in Church," she would say.

Suddenly Remick nudged me and pointed down. I leaned across his map case and saw we were flying directly over a cocoa-colored stream describing a lazy S through the elephant grass.

"Look at those fuckers," he said, and spat.

We were now very close to the ground, forty or fifty feet. Two Vietnamese were punting frantically at the edge of the river, trying to hide themselves and their boat, a kind of distended coracle, beneath the elephant grass on the bank.

"Fuckin' VC. Boat's half drowned in B-40 rounds."

The chopper swung back and hovered over the spot where the boat had gone to ground, close enough that the rotor-wash whipped the surface of the river in great coruscating ripples, their froth seeming to hiss as we dropped lower and lower. Remick now slammed the heel of his hand into the copilot's helmet, and when the co-pilot turned around he shook his wrist for him to look, like a doctor impatiently trying to bottom down a thermometer. I felt the helicopter sidling unevenly out from above the riverbank, at the same time catching a glimpse of the prow of the boat pitching under us and the two matted cone hats of the Vietnamese.

"Lower, goddammit."

The pilot pulled pitch, we sunk lower, and at the same time Remick and the right door gunner began firing. The Vietnamese were waving desperately, their mouths frozen open in their screams. The rounds tore forward, a hideous throaty staccato of hot scarlet. They stitched across the water and then they took the Vietnamese both at the same time, spinning and tumbling them crazily, one somersaulting backwards under the grass, the other sliding into the depth of the boat. The gunwale caught him by the underarm and draped his arm over the side.

"Like fuckin' Marat, that one!" Remick cried. "Now sink the goddamn boat."

"VC?" I shouted at him. "You sure?"

"Whaddya think they are, water nymphs? Boat that low's fulla one thing and one thing only. It ain't bananas, either." Remick spat again, and the door gunner sank the boat.

"You wanna go down and look it over?"

"No time, Adams."

So we climbed away from the riverbank, flying back towards the west, in the direction of the base camp. Abruptly the plain became jungle and the canopy again spread out under us, wetly viridian, quiet, impenetrable and unruffled. Remick leaned back against the bulkhead, folded his hands in his lap, and looked at us. I felt a crinkling in my pocket and took out Marjorie's letter. It was postmarked Far Hills, and it was my first letter from her in three weeks:

> Mark darling, we are all fine, incl the children and both cats. They miss you vy badly, as we all do, but your father-in-law is standing in quite nicely for you. Carol Renfrew took me to a lecture on decoupage two days ago at Red Bank State Teachers College, which you wd sneer at, I imagine, as being too tacky for anyone to be lectured about anything in. After the spiel on decoupage we went to a peace rally, just to watch it (of course!) and later wound up sitting in Gormans' having a beer with five or six people from the college. Carol told them you were in the Army and in Vietnam, and one of the men — a professor of classics, I think, asked what you were, an officer or E.M.? I told him you were an officer and he said that that was infinitely more

disgraceful, because you could resign whenever you wanted, and that you didn't have to fight in Vietnam if you didn't want to. Is that right? He asked what kind of work you were doing, and I told him about your getting cinder-block to rebuild the schoolhouse in Cai Tre, and of your admiration for John Rosenberg's "soldiers must know the value of what they have to destroy" article in *Encounter*. Well, he said, your husband may be civilized and humane, but I hope the hell he's not only civilized but also strong enough that when he sees these American soldiers shooting up civilians or people whose status he can't determine he's got enough guts to make them desist or report them, or whatever one does in the military. He said he was fully prepared to admit not all soldiers were Attila the Hun and he seemed impressed when I told him you'd been at Cambridge reading history. He said it was an officer's mission in a corrupt war to be subversive, to be an honest doubter (! Guess where he heard that. By reading your hero Basil Willey on Matthew Arnold). Carol told him you were a gentleman, splitting the word in half, a gentle man. "As long as he's strong, too," the man replied. Later he asked me out, and for the first time in my life I had a good comeback — no, I can wait until a *real* man gets home, which is only, what, eight weeks? We can stand on our heads for eight weeks, as you said. Be strong, darling, but be compassionate and kind. I am gratified it's not *your* Division that's cutting off people's ears or flying around like Maharajahs on howdah, shooting at anything that moves. The children look wonderful, they're *us*. I love you. The Naked Marja.

Colonel Hanks met the chopper and walked with us to the GP tent where the radios were set up. He seemed rested and jovial. For the first time in my ten months in his battalion he clapped me on the shoulder familiarly. He put his taut bronze face close to mine and kneaded the back of my neck with his fingers. "Got a question for you, Adams." He stopped and we all stopped and looked at him. "Here it is. You think Major Remick here's got it in him to command a battalion? You been

out with him a few times, you know his military mind."
Hanks shot Remick a mock stern glance, a teacher appraising an apt pupil. How 'bout it, Adams? Give us you ole fixed oh-pinion."

I knew Major Remick was on the current lieutenant colonels' promotion list, that his elevation to this plateau was imminent, and that it would make him eligible to command an infantry battalion. From the tone of Hanks's voice and the determined familiarity with which he had greeted me I reckoned that he had perhaps had a radio transmission while we were out flying around on "howdah," and that Remick must have been the subject of the transmission. Perhaps Remick had made light colonel that very day and a higher headquarters wanted him to command a battalion immediately. This was the *ne plus ultra* for professional officers in Vietnam — command of an infantry battalion. They lusted for it as, I suppose, Mr. Semple had once lusted after an embassy.

We had resumed our stroll to the tent. I stared at Major Remick for a second, watching him pick at his teeth with a blade of grass. He and Hanks and the sergeant major were all looking at me.

I stopped and looked at Remick and spat. "Best officer I ever served with, colonel. He'll command a battalion almost as well as you."

"Good," said Colonel Hanks, "real good." The following morning he left us to take up a new assignment at CORDS, and Lieutenant Colonel Remick took over our battalion. Our body-count rose sharply, and the last I heard of Remick was that he had made the early list to colonel, too. But we have not stayed in touch.

23

I was discharged from the Army in the fall of 1967, having, as the Army put it, "tendered" my resignation; and until my mother's unexpected death made it possible for us to move to Manhattan, into her old apartment, Marjorie and I lived in Hornebury, Connecticut, where, after a fashion, I taught English at the Grierson School. Lay down your rejuvenative bloodymary any Sabbath morning, gentle reader, and turn to the last two or three pages of the Sunday *Times Magazine* and you will see the school's anxious notices:

> *GRIERSON:* Boys with special problems turned into MEN, college acceptance guaranteed. Richly forested campus, indoor hockey-rink, eleven bldgs., etc. Contact Walter Kennard, Headmaster, Box 404, Hornebury, Conn. ENTER TO LEARN. GO FORTH TO SERVE. Founded 1923.

We lived in an apartment in a dormitory, jointly responsible for the welfare and deportment of forty boys, not counting our own children, to whose number a third was added in April, 1970.

For "special problems" read naked irredeemable stupidity. Occasionally we would have to deal with a fairy or a pothead or an arsonist (one of whom, two months after we left Grierson, burnt our former residence to the ground), but mainly we served — I borrow a phrase of opprobrium from Colonel Hanks — numbnubs, defective issue of New York and Philadelphia marriages, unwanted, snotty, dull, suspicious adolescents lately separated from schools like Hotchkiss and St. Mark's.

Of course the boys ogled Marjorie. The faculty, however, admired her for another reason: she was thought to have a special way with the boys and with the bored and distracted parents who came up to visit them once or twice a term, who came nosing onto our "richly forested" campus in Continental Mark III's and El Dorados, automobiles which, in honoring the DEAD SLOW signs on the campus roads, struck me as grotesquely perfect symbols for the parents' values. Not only that they were Mark III's or El Dorados; but that, cruising at four or five miles an hour when they could have shouldered angrily forward at eighty or ninety, they bespoke the terrible ennui and suppressed rage of their owners: their power, their impatience, their contempt for what the school claimed to stand for. One imagined these parents arguing in the cars as they glided silently onto the campus, already debating the best way to cut time off the return trip to New York. "Saw Mill River Parkway, my ass!" Occasionally I overheard them at football games: "Here, Mitzi, you got a twenty? I wannagivita Alex before we leave. Alex, commere, here's some dust for ya, old man. Now goddammit knuckle down and lemme see some A's on that next report."

I remember shrunken grandmothers dressed in black, following the parents around, patting the schoolboys on the backs of their heads and taking them aside and tell-

ing them how busy their fathers were; and the fathers,
their faces puce under skin-bronzers, talking in the ugly
inflections of New York Knick addicts, camel's hair
coated and sleek, holding narrow cigars like SS officers,
would say to me, "Whad kinda team you got this fall?
Gonna beat Hornecrest? They got black kids over there
at Hornecrest, scholarship kids. They can run."

I was not happy teaching at Grierson, and I'm not
sure why we stayed there so long. Yet Marjorie settled
easily and comfortably into that shabbily genteel little
world, made friendships rooted initially in admiration
for the other faculty wives, and later in ripening affection and shared — though largely imagined — hardship.
There was no public reappearance of her old fits of tem-
per. With perfect equanimity she listened to the masters'
debates about literature and history, leaning back smiling sweetly in their sofas, listening to their recordings of
baroque music. To all outward appearances she seemed
to have become what was then called a very together
woman, and I found myself almost hating her for it.

Why was this? Night after night I had lain awake in
Vietnam thinking about her, of the grim life I had sub-
jected her to in South Dakota, of my little cruelties to
her and my splenetic outbursts in the mornings. Like
every other married officer I knew in Vietnam, I resolved
that my homecoming would represent a new beginning,
the start of a honeymoon that would never end. Marjorie
and I would make gentle love night after night; she
would conceive babies on frosty Christmas Eves; we
would breakfast cheerily together in the bright mornings and ignore the petty frictions of marriage. We
would live for our children and our life would be an
idyll.

The reality was nothing like this. After a few months at Grierson our marriage evolved into a sort of armed truce, with its own demilitarized zones, its peculiar raids and forays and terror tactics: with everything but full-scale attacks. Peace talks would be suspended, then re-convened. Weeks would pass without trouble; then some gritty irritant would set things off again, and we would escalate. All measures short of war.

I would straggle in off the Thirds' soccer field where I had been coaching, bent on gin and tonic and Cronkite, to be brought up short by the presence of Willoughby Lubbock or Percy Younghusband or Jerzy Schwartz in our living room, usually in my chair. Across from him Marjorie would be sitting on a hassock, like a courtier hanging on Louis XIV's words, listening to some wild tale of cruelty or alienation, counseling the student gently and asking him, for Christ's sweet sake, to return to her whenever his work or his roommate was troubling him. She appeared to love doing this, and I conceived that she was doing it because she knew it antagonized me.

I would throw my cleats onto the cluttered floor of the hallway and go straight to the kitchen to make my-self a drink. Two or three minutes later she would come in to stand next to me and put her arm around my waist. "What kind of a day have you had, darling?" she would ask, day after day.

And I would tell her to get that snot-nose out of my living room, the last thing I wanted to see at the end of the day was some sniveling little fourth-former sucking up to my wife, lusting impossibly after those glorious bazaams. "Your cheap thrill, and don't give me that weeping willow routine."

Marjorie would move to the pantry and I would hear a sniffle. She would recompose herself, turn silently to face me, and say quietly, "You bastard."

"Don't bastard me. I teach these little morons four hours a day. I run around their stinking soccer field from four to six. I eat half my greasy meals with them. Keep them the hell out of this miserable flat."

"You don't teach them, you're no more a teacher than a gorilla. You're a martinet, a pedant in love with the sound of your own voice!" And then, inevitably: "If you were any kind of a teacher *or* a scholar we wouldn't be here. You'd be at Harvard writing books, making a reputation for yourself and giving us a decent life. You think I like this place? You think I grew up like this?"

"Shaadup!"

Yet at this point we would always reach out, or rather grope for each other, never looking each other in the face. We would stand holding each other, wondering if Wildeacre in the front room had heard us, looking around at the ugly little kitchen with its gimcrack deal furniture and its curling linoleum. I would kiss Marjorie once or twice and slap her on the bottom and promise to take them all to the drive-in. "Oh, darling," she would say. "Why do we do this to each other?" This would ruin it, but I'd keep up the pretense at rapprochement; invariably she would brighten quickly, and we'd have a decent evening together. Then the cycle would repeat itself.

The wonder of it was that things never seemed to get much worse. In that closed and suspicious community, we were never found out. As far as the rest of the faculty were concerned the Adamses were a happy couple, wonderfully suited to each other and to boarding-school life, each with an enviable vocation. We jogged along, oddly sustained and comforted by the notion that all marriages were like ours. I suppose they are.

Late in the spring of 1971 I failed Cabot Calhoun on his English final exam. Since Calhoun had taken a failing average into the exam, I failed him for the course, too; this made it impossible for him to graduate.

In a school whose very life depended on its attractiveness to retreads, to boys who had been eliminated from decent schools for one thing or another, young Calhoun had distinguished himself as a boy who had arrived at Grierson at thirteen and stayed the whole course. He was immensely popular with his classmates and the younger boys; he was a prefect; the faculty admired him; he had captained football and track and he had gained — his low grades in English notwithstanding — early acceptance at Penn and Michigan. He was a slender, graceful young man with an affecting unshorn cowlick hanging over his left eye — something that caused him to toss his head four or five times a minute, like a stallion shucking flies. So far as I knew, he had given no one any trouble.

Alas, as I once found it necessary to write on the efficiency report of one of my lieutenants, "he had a dull mind."

Inevitably I was sent for by the headmaster and asked to administer a re-exam. Dr. Phelps said he would abide my decision on pass or failure, but that in all fairness to the boy's family and to the boy himself, he deserved another chance. I did not object and I set Calhoun a two-page paper, half multiple-choice, half essay.

The first portion of the exam he bombed cold. He had Balzac being born in Dove Cottage and Shakespeare writing "Bound East for Cardiff." Hemingway had written "A Rose for Emily" and Thomas Wolfe had married a southern girl called Zelda Sayre. Only a B-plus on the essay could have saved Calhoun now; anything less meant than he would not graduate with his class — which meant the draft would get him, and he'd be sent to Vietnam, probably, and . . . I could see the tears in his parents' eyes as I read his paper:

> Frost's "Stopping by Woods on a Snowy Evening." Here Frost sommuned forth remebrance of his own New England exposure, objectafying it in a single scene in which he is apparently riding in a sleigh, going home from visiting someone and the sleigh stopped in the woods, causing the horse to wonder why they had stopped at all, it being very cold that time of year in New England — as well we know! The poet looks around him at the woods and reflects how lovly "dark and deep" they are but that sitting there isn't going to get him very far in life, and that it *is* very cold sitting there. He had promised his wiffe to get home on time, maybe for Xmas Eve. So he let forth a giddiap! and they tootled on home. Pass me, Sir.

I failed Calhoun again. Dr. Phelps backed me up. Calhoun did not graduate that June.

"You cruel, cruel man," Marjorie said.

"Hardly cruel, my dear woman. You saw his paper. He'd be the last kid from Grierson Penn would ever accept. No, the reverse of cruel. It was an intelligent and decent thing to do."

"Decent!" Marjorie stood with her back to the window shaking her head slowly. Behind her I could see the heavy cars discharging their passengers — happy parents who were arriving for graduation week. "You've got all the equipment but a heart," she said.

"You've got all the equipment but a brain."

We fought again and made another truce. Calhoun's father was perhaps the motive force behind my dismissal from the faculty of Grierson School, which occurred two weeks later, the day my mother's will was finally probated. I would have left anyway, I think. We moved to New York; and hearing one night at a party the "Ceremony of Lessons and Carols — Christmas Eve at King's College, Cambridge," decided to spend what the New York radio and TV announcers, not wanting to offend the Chosen People, call "The Holidays," in England. As an *acquit de conscience* I decided to do some research there, too — for a biography of an English military man whose *Reminiscences* I'd once read in that grim second autumn in Cambridge eight years before, Sir Gordon Sandstone.

THREE

Mark

24

Mr. Frederick Giles's reputation in the Rufus Arms thickened rapidly — I say "thicken" because it was impossible to determine at that early stage what the people I had met in the hotel really thought of him. Already I was anxious to get Carstairs off in a corner some evening and start him talking about his guest, who, you will remember, had stayed in the hotel many times before. But there was no chance for that, as Carstairs was off with the Mid-Surrey Hunt when I got in from London the day after Giles's drunken harangue. Meantime, however, his performance had mysteriously come to enjoy a wide currency. I imagine this owed mainly to the barmaid, Susan, who had given anyone who cared to listen a most favorable report of what she had understood to be a great paean to the vanished glories of England: as exemplified in Giles's proposing the health of Lord Nelson. (Susan as a rule sat behind the partition separating the bar from the pantry when she was not making drinks.) "It sometimes takes them Yanks to remind us how great England was, and still is," she explained to people.

Marjorie told me that the gentleman-swineherd, Faricy, had talked, too, over his lunch of pork-roll and stout in the pub. Though he had dismissed Giles rather curtly as a bounder, he had qualified this judgment by adding that he *was* amusing, and that he had considered his niece's person in all respects superior to that of any Gainsborough heroine.

It had been an unseasonably warm day, almost tepid and somewhat enervating. We were both tired again, Marjorie from entertaining the children, I from several hours' uninspiring drudge-work in the Museum in London. We decided to have dinner in the hotel and go to the pub afterwards. Marjorie warned me to be on my good behavior — otherwise she would make a public stink. "Go ahead," I told her, "make a public stink, it won't do me any harm."

"There will be no repeats of last night," she declared, and she put the tip of her forefinger on my lips and I kissed it. "Got me?"

"Do you make yourself perfectly clear?"

"Do I?"

"Where's my stinking foulard necktie?"

But I wanted nothing so much as a repeat of last night. I was intrigued by Giles: by the bizarre eclecticism of his fund of historical and political opinions, by the rumbustious attitudes he struck and the cocksureness of his pronouncements. I had egged him on, perhaps, and had gotten my deserts, but he did not strike me as the kind of man who cultivated grudges. And by now I could see he liked Marjorie, and that she felt a kind of sympathy for him.

In setting down this account of our encounters with Frederick Giles and of the things they were leading us to, I am reminded of a conversation I had with him out in the garden of the hotel one morning before breakfast. It was chilly, and we paced up and down on the short walkway between the dining room and the garage to keep warm, Giles swinging his arms in wide arcs at his sides to get his circulation going. "You know," he said,

"I was once really struck by an obituary I read." I asked him whose it was and he replied: "The Dominican gigolo's — Porfirio Rubirosa's."

For whatever light it may cast on Giles's character, I summarize what he said about the famous lover.

The obituary claimed that Rubirosa's monstrous successes with women owed to his ability to isolate them from their surroundings, to give them the impression that his attentions were so intensely focused on them that they could feel they were the only things that had ever mattered to him. One by one, of course, they felt this. Woman's monogamous, man's polygamous, ha-ha! Porfirio Rubirosa had an extraordinary gift, the gift of the born lover, or, come to think of it, the born politician, a gift without which no one could get very far in any "interpersonal endeavor."

"Did you ever see the son-of-a-bitch?" Giles asked.

Only in the papers, I said. I had a vague recollection of Rubirosa driving a Maserati into an oak tree in the Champs-Élysées, little more than that.

"Yeah, that's right, but remember how greasy he was? But what you thought was greasy, Adams, that wasn't what women thought about, not the women he got it in his head to seduce. They only saw a man who totally worshiped them, who was prepared to do anything for *their* good. Remember what he looked like? Now, if you looked like that you had to have something, didn't you?"

I waited for Giles to tell me how well hung Rubirosa was, which he did, even anticipating my next question about how he, Giles, might have come by such an arcane bit of knowledge, by asserting that "damn near everybody knows that." And he went on to tell me that Rubirosa's was nothing; that, hell, he had been in the FBI

Museum in Washington, where Dillinger's root was kept on permanent display, pickled in formalin, right in the lobby of the building for everyone to see. "Go to Washington and see it, you don't believe me. Dillinger was *pawn-dawn kay chevelle*."

"You mean *pendant comme un cheval?*"

"Yeah. Hung like a horse. Twenty-six inches long."

But we had strayed off the main point, which was that we could all learn something from this son-of-a-bitch Rubirosa. Whether we wanted to or not, we had to take our hats off to him. "He didn't just chat them up," Giles stressed. "He made them feel desired, and loved, too." This was what counted in the game of life; this was Rubirosa's unknowing legacy. "You talk to somebody, no matter who it is, you make them think they're the only thing you're interested in, sexual or otherwise. You start everyone off this way in any case, because you can't tell what you'll wind up wanting from them." And all the while, Giles was giving me an object lesson in Rubirosan interpersonal relations by craning his neck and staring at me while we walked back and forth in the garden. He spoke very slowly and with deliberation, almost as though he foresaw that I would soon have opportunities to apply the lessons he had imparted.

Then, as a coda, in a typically Gilesian form of summation which introduced new, unanswerable evidence: "Also remember what Lord Chesterfield says about not talking about yourself. Just draw people out. Let them do the talking. Then, when you've got them, and you don't like what you hear, splat!" Giles slammed the back of his right hand into the palm of his left — not a satisfactory gesture this time, as it loosened the expansion-band of his multi-dialed chronometer, causing it to slide over the heel of his hand.

"Got me?"

"I gotcha, Frederick," I said.

Ten or twelve people sat drinking that night at the tables along the walls of the pub — four other couples besides Marjorie and me, including a young barrister from Liphook and his date, who sat around Lord Nelson's table with us. This, I imagined, was where Marjorie and Giles ate their lunches, and the regulars in the pub indulged us, or seemed to indulge us, by not using the table when we were there. A thrill for the Americans, they must have thought.

And since the table lay to the immediate right of the entranceway Giles didn't see us when he first came in. Instead he walked directly to the bar. He wore his smoking jacket, but the belt had been removed. On his spare frame it hung like a medieval tabard.

"Susan," he cried out, "bring whiskey-soda."

She was in the pantry and did not appear right away. Giles called her again: "Bwana, bring whiskey-soda!" He drummed idly with his fingers on the bar and turned to face his audience wearing an expression like a stand-up comic's feigning disgust with a straightman in the orchestra. Susan finally hove into view from behind the partition, wiping her hands on the apron she wore over a velours muumuu.

"Yes, Mr. Giles?"

"Y'ever read'ny Hemingway, Susan?"

"Heard of him."

"His people used to yell that at their bearers when

they'd get in from hunting. But it had an affectionate ring to it."

"What was that?"

"Bwana, whiskey-soda."

"Yes?"

Poor Giles. This was the kind of thing that made me genuinely sorry for him. I don't think he meant to offend people. Probably he was sensitive enough to imagine the inflections in the voices of the white hunters. They meant no humiliation of their servants. That his relationship to a part-time barmaid was hardly analogous to a big-game hunter's with his gunbearer never occurred to him.

"I'm not your bearer, sir," the girl said gently.

"Of course you're not, honey! Here," he said, "keep the change." And he handed her some paper, probably a pound note. This only made things worse, but Susan took the money and said nothing. He watched her walk away, shook his head and spun around on the rickety barstool he was sitting on.

"Bwana!" I said to him.

"Yes, indeed, Bwana. But he wrote better things than *The Green Hills of Africa,* a hell of a lot better things than that." So saying, and to the manifest puzzlement of the barrister, he came over to us. I pushed a chair at him and introduced our guests.

"What were you?" he said to Coleman. "Oxford or Cambridge?"

"Cambridge," Coleman answered. He was a man of perhaps twenty-six or twenty-seven with pale silky hair and the shadow of an unsuccessful moustache on his lip. We had known him only twenty minutes.

Giles rose halfway out of his chair; he put out his

hand, palm-downward, calling for silence. "Ah" — he rasped — "Fair Cambridge. The Fitzwilliam. King's College Cathedral. The Punts — or is it the Banks? Didn't they work on the atom in Cambridge during the war?"

Coleman started to answer but Giles went on.

"Is King's still full of fairies? You know, the old head-master of King's was the last man known to have slept with Rupert Brooke. But he died in the blitz. Did you make that show?"

That show. I looked at Marjorie, but she was looking at Giles.

"I was born in 1944," Coleman answered. He looked shyly at Marjorie and me, wondering if it was all a joke.

Giles pressed right ahead. "I am curious about this fairy business. It is a question that deserves serious ventilation." Then he redeemed himself somewhat: "You are not a graduate of King's College, are you, sir?"

"No, I'm not."

"I could tell."

"Thank God," Coleman said with a forgiving laugh.

"No, but I'll give you my theory about all that business. I think such perversions are probably rooted in the hothouse atmosphere of your public schools. What happens is that they are run by young bachelors of limited means whose duties make it hard for them to get off-campus. So they turn on their charges, and their charges turn on themselves. A lot of the boys are confirmed pederasts by the time they leave those schools."

Thus the issue was ventilated. What was I supposed to do with guests I knew might have to meet Giles? Warn them in advance, and spoil the sport? Or let them have him cold turkey and risk the consequences? It was too late now.

"Is that not so?" Giles asked.

"Alas, quite so," said Coleman obligingly. He could play, too. "Indeed the governance of England is the province of the confirmed pederast."

Giles laughed. "When do you take silk? Didn't Mark say you were a barrister?"

"Not before I can disencumber myself of my heterosexual habits."

"Touché, touché. You can see I'm not being serious. Yet those schools are founts of perversion, are they not?"

"But of course."

"Which was your school?"

"Shrewsbury."

"Ah, Shrewsbury."

"You know it?"

"Yes, indeed. A munificent foundation. What would you do in those schools? What would you read there? What Roman authors?"

The conversation appeared to grow serious. "Well, it's been some years," Coleman answered. "I remember the *Gallic War.*"

"Remember that goddamned bridge they built that we had to translate?"

Coleman nodded. The bridge. The tripartite division of Gaul. Vercingetorix.

"I thought that was good, the way Caesar put himself in the third person."

"Was clever of him, wasn't it?" Our guest had taken Giles's measure rapidly. Meantime Giles had begun studying Coleman's friend, a thin unsmiling albino. "You know what the third person is?" he asked her.

"I think so."

"Marjorie?"

"No, Mr. Giles. What's the third person?"

What was it in her voice that gave me my clue, warned me that such a question did not entail the same purpose, was not asked in the same spirit in which Marjorie's acerb comments, her malicious pinpricking observations had been offered the night before? Of course she knew what the third person was. Somehow the question sounded prearranged, a kind of plant, a part of some gulling scheme to make me think Marjorie's apparent contempt for Giles persisted.

Those black dazzling eyes of his fastened on her like limpets, as if he too were trying to show by his expression that he saw she was trying to make a fool of him. Of course I was fooled by them. "Here we go again," I thought. But he only sighed, regathered himself and explained what the third person meant.

"Why, thank you, Mr. Giles." Marjorie said.

Giles looked at Coleman. "What else would you read?"

Well, they had done Caesar, also Suetonius and Livy — which last, Giles broke in, contained the filthy passage about Nero.

"And what kind of English Lit would you have there?" he asked.

"Oh, you know, Chaucer and Tennyson. Thackeray."

"Not one of them could hold a candle to Goncharov," Giles said grinning.

"To *whom?*"

"To Ivan Goncharov." (He even pronounced it Ee-vawn.) "He was a Russian author of the last century, a very good author. He wrote a long book called

Oblomov in which a man tries to get out of bed for five hundred pages."

No one said anything. None of us had ever heard of Goncharov, and I for one was not in the mood for discussing the world's classics.

Coleman didn't know about last night. He sensed Giles was embarrassed that no one had taken him up on his statement. "And who would you put next to him?"

"Well, he's never been properly translated anyway," Giles answered.

"Well who would you put number one, Frederick?" said Marjorie.

"Ernie Pyle."

"What kind of crap is this?" I asked him.

"Don't you dare patronize me, Adams. I was reading Ernie Pyle when you were in your bloody bassinet."

"That makes him a good writer, does it?"

Again: the curt sideways nod, a meld of contempt and exasperation, aimed at me while he looked at Marjorie, and while he made a *Whadya do with somebody like this?* gesture with both hands.

"Christ, go on, man," I said to him. "We're all ears."

"Assholes and elbows," he muttered.

He was not easily mollified. I imagined him smashing a Guinness bottle on the table and holding it at my throat, trying to force me to acknowledge the greatness of Ernie Pyle.

Yet, in response to some unspoken warning (I imagined this, too) from Marjorie, he backed off. Calmly he arranged his glass and ashtray like a student setting up for an evening's work. Now he folded his hands and stared at Coleman. And before he launched into another of his silly harangues I saw my wife reach across the table and pat him gently on the back of his hand, as if to reassure him of her support, no matter what he might say. Forgive my husband, he's obtuse. He hates everyone.

Down the sluice we went.

What we had to do, Giles explained, was to "rank authors" not only in terms of the excellence of their published writing, but also in terms of the conditions under which they wrote. Now, we should take Pyle. OK? Here was an author who wrote on a battered Remington in a foxhole, or in the well-deck of an LST pitching around on the Pacific, a badly named ocean since they really have serious storms there and which was, furthermore, three times as wide as the little gulch that separated England from her lost colonies. ("Take no offense, Mr. Coleman.") And furthermore Pyle was sick damn near all the time with amoebic dysentery, a disease which made it excruciatingly difficult for him to concentrate on his work, since he was constantly having to get up.

Ha-ha, if we got his drift.

But here we had in fact arrived at the very core of Pyle's genius. He had a common touch that Tolstoy, who was a duke or count, or Proust — who was a pansy — or Stephen Crane, who never even went to war, couldn't begin to approach. See, Pyle would get down in there and mix it up with Rawlins, Wyoming, or Bangor, Maine, which was where those soldiers were from whose feats he commemorated in writings as fine as anything written before Agamemnon, or since.

OK? And he had one *hell* of a prose style, too. It was "pellucid" because it came direct from the heart with no monkey-business to get between the writer and us. It *was* honest. It was subject and predicate prose. Eventually the critics would give Pyle his just due, but we would none of us live that long. And there was another criteria we had to use. Pyle was *read* — unlike, say, Scott F. Fitzgerald or Arthur Schlesinger, and what the masses had that left-wing professors and society blowhards didn't have was a true sense of what was good and what was rotten — which 98 percent of the writing in our own times was. Rotten. Good writing you felt in the gut, like good paintings.

Marjorie smiled at that, of course. I waited for her to nudge me with her foot, but she did not. Giles had meantime finished, and in impatient masturbatory gestures was running his closed fist up and down the unknotted fawn necktie he wore, between his American flag and his throat. Now he opened his eyes wide enough to crease his forehead and craned forwards over the table and glared at me.

"Do I make my point?"

Coleman humored him along, wondering aloud where he could get a "collected works of Mr. Pyle."

"Maybe I'll send you one."

"You *are* kind."

Even as he sipped at his drink I could tell Giles was cranking himself up for another long harangue, but his animosity for me, which had seemed to issue from him like a vapor, had vanished.

"Yeah, but don't expect a lot of legal jargon in it. May I buy you a drink?"

"Thank you," said Coleman.

Usually when Giles said he wanted to buy you a drink it meant that he wanted you to listen to him talk while you drank it. I fully expected that whatever he chose to say next would be aimed at Coleman who — despite his courtesy — had treated him with the same cavalier in-difference, the same ironic amusement, I probably had the night before.

You know David Coleman, what he is, what he repre-sents, if you've spent any time in England. Giles might rage silently against him as he had roared out his hatred for Princeton, etcetera, last night. They say that Hitler foamed and boiled when he heard Churchill's voice; that the Kaiser often alternately raged and wept when he discussed the English aristocracy; that Napoleon sought for assurances that he could live in the country like an English gentleman when that country, which he had affected to despise, finally got its hands on him. I loved England, but I couldn't be an Englishman, and didn't want to be. Giles in a way did. Thus, while he had held up Philippa as the symbol of what he imagined we wanted for ourselves, embarrassing her with his gro-tesque compliments, would he not be likely to rage at Coleman?

The first thing that strikes you about this Coleman type is his character, which combines diffidence and self-possession in about equal degrees. In conversation it manifests itself as puckishness: "It was clever of Caesar, wasn't it?"

Englishmen like Coleman are born into the families of the country gentry. They first have ponies and read Beatrix Potter. Their fathers are stern and remote, their mothers immoderately lovely. When they are six or seven they are packed off to the Dragon, grow tough and sinewy playing soccer in the searing English cold, parse their Caesar — as Coleman told Giles — and after a few years arrive with dirty collars at Shrewsbury or

Harrow or Eton, where friendship and respect come to them without their seeming to seek them. There they learn to write a simple British sentence by conning Homer and Livy. Quietly they become authorities on most matters; at the same time, because they are implicitly conscious of who they are, they are unlikely to have accepted their schoolmasters' views on politics and the humane letters; so that, when they are asked polite social questions about such subjects, and impolite ones as well, their answers tend either to be devastatingly to the point, or to uncover utterly unexpected hollows of ignorance. There are treacherous snares for those putting the questions, and Giles would find this out shortly.

One of the most brilliant students of military history I ever knew — he was a fellow of Pembroke, Cambridge — took me aside three years ago at a reunion in New York.

"What dyew think of that squabble in South Aziah? In Veet-nahm?"

I was staggered to think this eminent and gentle scholar was so immersed in his study of the feudal system in Normandy that he could have failed to notice our agony in Indochina. I even mimicked his pronunciation to his face: Yes, our chaps were in Veet-nahm just then. They had been in Korea with your Gloucester-chaps and now they were in Veet-nahm.

"Ah," he said, "but I hear the Westmoreland multi-battalion offensive falters. Not enough air support this time of year. The typhoon would have set in by now, I should have thought?"

I steered him onto that summer's Wimbledon.

Anyway, these Coleman types have gotten at their

subjects from odd perspectives, and have thought about them with an odd mix of flippancy and rigor.

Well. Then they would leave their Harrow or wherever and pass quietly along to Christ Church or Magdalen at Oxford or to that exquisite citadel of pederasty which Giles imagined was King's, Cambridge. Often they would be good at games, as they say, though never dreaming of training too hard for them. They would tend also to be readers of nineteenth century fiction; the politics and economics they were supposed to be studying would get into their heads in other ways. And on weekends they would not be seen about the college. They had gone, you would be told, to Blythehaven or Carinmore, names you supposed identified their parents' houses or the titles of peers whose daughters they were seeing in Kensington. And on the Monday following, as you and one of their number sat for a joint tutorial, and after you had heard the don tell you that your essay sounded like something out of the American magazine *Time*, this yawning young leopard would read a piece that sounded as though it had been xeroxed out of the *English Historical Review*; and then he and the don would debate it earnestly for an hour while you listened mesmerized to them. You would later find out the English student had written his paper in the boathouse during a squall.

Invariably our prototype, to make him singular, would leave Cambridge with a dazzlingly good degree or at least with an Upper Second: if the latter, you could infer he had done no work to speak of in his three years, but that he had read enough Trollope to convince the examiners that he knew almost as much history as they did. They might have been bothered by a certain arrant flippancy in his writing; perhaps he had called Queen Victoria a "splendid creature," or begun his answer with the phrase, "The trouble with this question is that it fails to . . ."

Then he would disappear, driving out of Cambridge in the thirty-year-old Morgan he had rebuilt one summer at home when he was bored. You would hear later that he had passed first into the Treasury and was about to marry an immoderately lovely woman, a distant cousin, the daughter of a brigadier in Kircudbrightshire, this Coleman, leaving in his quiet wake a thousand dancing fragments of puzzled or devastated personalities with whom he had crossed wits or joined in a pub for a few drinks.

An idealized portrait of a breed now inevitably disappearing? Possibly. Yet as I sat studying him from across the table I seemed to recognize in him what I admired about England and Englishmen — and, despite what happened in the next few minutes, I still feel the same towards him.

Giles returned with the drinks, making a show of serving Marjorie first. The fool had laid a folded bar towel across his forearm, and he served her off a pewter tray. "Pearls goeth before the swine," he said, looking at Coleman and me.

"*Thank* you, Frederick," Marjorie said. "You *are* kind." But he had already disappeared through the entranceway.

Now I heard his voice again and I looked around the edge of the partition and saw him coming down the stairs into the lobby with Mrs. Admiral Carleton-Whyte, an elegant and dusty widow who had lived in the hotel for many years. From the way he looked he might have been escorting a vial of nitroglycerine; she and other old ladies like her, I gathered, were part of the constituency he had been trying to develop in the hotel. He wanted them to think of him as their 'umble servant, their quiet American. If the conversation I overheard was any index to his success in this enterprise, however, I am afraid his efforts were largely unavailing.

They came very slowly down the stairs, pausing above each stair like mourners in delay-step in a funeral march. Giles walked on her left, and his left hand cupped her crooked arm while his right arm encircled her waist, though not quite touching her. It was as though he imagined she might pitch backwards like a puppet jerked by strings from the overhanging balcony. The old lady was talking about a painting.

"We had a lovely still life Jeremy had got before I kniew him. It was a Stranover, a Dutchman, don't you know, who had come over with Lely. A lovely old thing. But it had this great sort of fly at the surface of the melon. I couldn't bear it in our dining room."

"Ah, Stranover."

"Yes, he was a gorgeous painter. But we couldn't have that fly in our dining room."

"Of course not. You should have put the painting in a hallway with a lot of other still lifes. You can't have a still life with a fly on it looking at you when you eat."

And so on. By the time they had descended to the lobby floor, Mrs. Carleton-Whyte was defending the right of the fly to be in such a painting and the painting's fitness to hang anywhere she chose to put it. It had taken Giles just under a minute to rile her up.

He rejoined us, spreading his legs apart and yanking the top of his chair under his crotch, plunking himself down in a little half-leap. Then he teetered gingerly back and folded his arms across his chest. "I like old bats," he said. "You have your best friendships with women past the hot-flash period of their lives . . . Where were we?"

25

"I had just been instructed in the difficulty of getting Pyles," Coleman said.

"They're not as hard to come by as you think!"

"Funny fellow," I said to Giles.

"Where were we? — yes, we were discussing writers." Giles addressed Coleman. "Were you a sporting man, sir?"

"A bit, nothing to speak of."

"A rowing man, sir?"

"I've had a boil or two in my day."

"I am an Anglophile, Mr. Coleman, and I hope you will not take offense at the question I am about to pose, because I believe in the natural consanguinity of the English-speaking peoples. However, I will still put the question to you: How do you account for the natural primacy of American over English crews? Wait. Let me answer for you, and then you speak to my answer — OK?" Off he went.

The primacy was natural enough if you considered some of the following factors: the size of the American, and certainly the Russian oarsmen as well, both of whom had enjoyed the benefit of orange juice and raw wheat germ from early youth. In Russia they had a place called Georgia, where the dialectical materialist Khrushchev was from, whose oranges were excelled as to size only by those of our own Florida, and as to flavor only by those of California. Besides, the river currents were stronger in America, and the rivers themselves wider and rougher. Americans could strengthen themselves rowing against the current. "That's what puts muscle on your back and gets the thighs hard as rocks."

Also there was the fantastic native determination of the American postadolescent, his spirit that thrived on competition and would take on all comers. He daresaid Coleman had never seen an English crew row down an American boat.

But Giles had stepped into a deeper and more treacherous current than he knew.

"As a matter of fact, my dear fellow, I saw that very thing last summer at Henley. Leander rowed down [Leander was an English rowing club, and "rowing down" meant catching up with, and beating another crew] a Harvard eight and beat them by a length . . ."

Giles twisted his face into a kind of Churchillian pout. "Harvard," he said. "You know what Harvard is?"

"Quite decent university, I should have thought."

"Decent my foot."

"No, you are wrong, sir. It is an excellent university. Founded, I believe, by a Cambridge man."

"Probably from King's College." Giles paused. "Adams, your wife tells me you went to Cambridge too — that right?"

I told him it was.

"Our own not good enough for you?"

"Just wanted to avoid Harvard," I said.

"Good answer, Big One." He turned back to Coleman. "Let me tell you a thing or two about Harvard University. You know what kinda people go there?"

Coleman affected to yawn.

"Queers. A lot of Jews, too. You got it in your head what a queer is?"

"Foolish thing for you to say. Of course there're queers in Harvard. There're queers in the University of Oxford and I daresay in Kansas State University as well. Your college, I understand."

"Who told you that?"

"Your friend here," Coleman said, nodding at me.

"Harvard's ninety percent queer. And it's a hundred percent left-wing."

"Perhaps some of the left-wingers are queer themselves?"

"Don't hassle me with syllogisms. You never heard of a first-class patriot coming out of Harvard."

"Kennedy?"

"Name me a patriotic act Kennedy ever did and I'll buy you a bottle of Jack Daniels. Susan, you got any Jack Daniels?" Susan looked over, confused. "Never mind. Name me a patriotic act of Kennedy."

"Well, he married Jackie."

"She's a polack."

"You're a fool."

"Wha-at?"

"I said you're a bloody fool. I don't think I've heard so much nonsense in my life."

"You may not agree with me, but don't call me a fool."

"You're a fool," Coleman said again, quietly, confidently supercilious. "We don't often see people like you here. Thank God for that. Why don't you go outside and shout your insults at the wind?"

"No one calls me a fool and gets away with it."

"I do. I reckon many people do. Who let you in here? Carstairs? I must have a talk with him."

The possibility of their fighting, of Giles going for Coleman, had passed early in this exchange, and Coleman knew it. He was now licensed to press his attack.

But of course he didn't. Instead he got up from the table with his date, reached down and picked up his drink, and, standing there, staring directly at Giles, finished it off. Then he turned to me.

"Good night, Adams. Awfully sorry about this. Seemed necessary, though. You must come out and see us. Marjorie, do remember to call us, will you?"

And so they left, Coleman stopping on the way out to say something to the barmaid I couldn't hear.

"Crow," Giles said, "I wasn't trying to stir him up or anything."

Whatever he had been trying to do, I told him, it had been a pretty shoddy performance. He disgusted me, and I told him I thought we'd had enough of him for one night.

For which he rewarded me with an *et tu Brute?* look of amazement and confusion. He was utterly crestfallen.

"Giles," I said to him, "you can't go around talking to people like this. Try a little circumspection."

"Nah," he shook his head, "that's your bag."

I asked Marjorie if she were coming upstairs with me.

"You go up to bed, Mark. I'll be up in a few minutes."

When I got outside the pub I motioned for her to excuse herself.

"What is it, Mark?"

"You coming?"

"I'll stay with him for a while."

"What for?"

"He needs understanding and help."

I told her I thought her friend was beyond helping.

"I don't know what gets into him . . . he's not like that when you're not around."

"Look," I said, "I can't help what he's like when I'm around or when I'm not around. But don't blame me for what happened tonight. It was all Coleman's doing. And he had plenty of cause, too."

"That man's a snob like you."

"Marjorie, look . . ."

"You go on up. I'll be up soon."

"You're a little soft on him, aren't you?"

"Good night, Mark." Her voice had menace in it. She turned from me and I saw her walk back towards him, towards where he sat staring at the table. Her hands were folded before her, and she walked with a slow, springy step like a schoolgirl in a processional. I saw Giles look up at her, and I saw in his face an expression of pure gratitude, and of relief and happiness. What was in hers? I could not see. She sat down where I had been sitting and looked at him for a long time, without saying anything.

I went upstairs. What Coleman had done to Giles was well worth having Marjorie waste her time commiserating with him. Perhaps now he knew his place.

26

Historians and writers are drawn to the craft of biography out of powerful curiosities about how their subjects got to be what they are remembered as being. Too often the great are remembered for the achievements of their maturity, for their behavior in times of crisis, for their frailties or strengths in those times and the honors or disgrace these led to. We do not remember Bismarck the young romantic, the writer of passionate love letters, the slim and foppish student with duelling scars on his jowlless cheeks. Gladstone is perpetually enshrined in the common consciousness as a sinewy and desiccated old man in a hurry. Was Dame Sitwell ever young? Was Robert E. Lee ever beardless? Did John Henry Newman, who came to cherish the "high intrinsic excellence of virginity," ever masturbate?

My general, Sir Gordon Sandstone, is remembered mainly for the coolness and finesse with which he planned and executed in Britain's wars of the later nineteenth century; he had what are known conventionally as very "clear" brains — the ability, rare in most military commanders, to grasp the essentials of a developing tactical situation and to formulate plans quickly, basing them on his understanding of those essentials. He also had — if I may quote Norman Mailer — that *sine qua non* of generalship: the ability "to translate will into immediate and effective action." There was almost no color in his personality save a certain jarring choler glimpsed only by a few members of his personal staff; nothing memorable in his dispatches. He held his soldiers' respect, but neither cultivated nor enjoyed their affection.

He is thus remembered by practically everyone but two or three cranky ancestors and a few scholars. He was the general who saved the day at Flattensburg, the battle from which his little force went forward to their great success at Pretoria. You may know the McCormack painting of Sandstone, which hangs in the National Portrait Gallery in London, and that is how everyone remembers Sandstone: a thin spare man with a gray and seamy face wearing dusty khaki and a pith helmet and sitting astride a sorrel at Duffer's Drift.

I had no powerful curiosity about Sandstone. When friends of Marjorie's had asked me in New York why I was going to write about him, women who had less interest in my answer to their question than I had in the subject of my biography, I told them simply "because he's there"; and what I told them was closer to the truth than they imagined. But I knew no one had written about the general, and I knew that his private papers, once the property of my college at Cambridge, had now been moved to the Army Museum at Chelsea. I had once written an essay about him my tutor had liked, in which I compared him to Walter Bedell Smith. The don remembered the essay because he had not known who Walter Bedell Smith was, and he arranged access to the papers for me through Sandstone's great-nephew. So much for motivation.

My work at the Museum was uncovering little to contradict the popular image of the general. I had his diaries and journals at my disposal, sixty-five letters written to his wife in Lincolnshire from Kandahar and later South

Africa, none of which antedated his promotion to colo-nel; five reports sent his parents by the headmaster of St. Neot's in the early 1860's, and some yellowing volumes of the official histories of the campaigns in which he had fought, and in which his troops, in his favorite phrase, had "done execution." One searched through all these materials in vain for any evidence that he was anything but a crusty, doughty, somewhat bloody-minded, cool, conventionally equipped British cavalry officer.

So my work went smoothly but without excitement or any particular satisfaction. By the end of my third afternoon at the Museum I had little left to do except prepare pages for the Xeroxer and make entries in my own notebooks — abstracts from Sandstone's letters, which were too frail for reproduction. I was going through the material perfunctorily; half the time I sat staring out at the dingy London afternoons thinking about Giles, wondering what he and Marjorie talked about at their lunches in the hotel with the children, chuckling — sometimes out loud — over his crazy views and tortuous modes of expressing himself. And now too I looked forward to having drinks with my former roommate at Cambridge, whom I had not seen since I left England in 1964.

David Ashley was frozen in my memory as he had been at twenty-two. We had lived together for eighteen months, and I continued to regard him as the best friend I ever had. We had drunk and worked and lived to-gether; once we had shared the same woman. When I last saw him he had been pathetically and violently drunk on bourbon, a whiskey that had enjoyed a small vogue in Cambridge when we were up. David couldn't handle bourbon. None of the English could, even on stomachs full of Brussels sprouts and kidney pie. I felt like a white trader in Parkman giving firewater to the Oglala Sioux.

Now he shared a flat in Moor Settles Place, just off Bayswater. He was a doctor, a practicing physician, unmarried and with no admiration for the high intrinsic excellence of virginity. In the years since we had left Clare we had had almost no contact at all. The one letter I had had from him reached me when I was with Colonel Hanks's battalion in Vietnam — a hurried scrawled note in which he crassly suggested that he had been attracted to the practice of medicine because it afforded him continuous opportunities to examine and palpitate — his word — the breast of the adult human female. I read the letter several times, enough times to discover that the first letters in the note's first eight sentences together spelled *fellatio*. It was almost impossible to imagine him practicing medicine.

"Mark, my dear fellow!"

"How are you, David?"

"Looking very fit, you are. Can you still get it up?"

"You gross man. Same as always."

"I'll get us a drink."

David's flatmate, another Cantabridgian whom David had known when we were up, was away on assignment for Burma Oil. The apartment didn't look much different from our set of rooms at Clare, except that it had a kitchen. It smelled of sausage and athletic socks, and was sparsely furnished in heavy dark Victorian tables and chairs. A tiny electric bar, orange and forlorn, provided the only heat.

Sounds of drawers being opened and slammed shut could be heard from the kitchen. Walking across the living room I noticed two bare feet hanging crazily over the arm of a sofa with its back towards me. I walked over and looked down.

"Hullo," said a girl. "You're Mark, aren't you?"

"Mark, yes. Who are you?"

"Friend of David's."

"You have a name?"

"Don't actually. I'm just a fixture here."

Such women had been fixtures in David's life at Cambridge. They were rarely introduced to you, and they almost never introduced themselves. I remembered them as always seeming to be standing up smoothing their skirts or opening windows.

"Margot — you want a sherry?"

"Fine, David."

"How long have you been here?" I asked her.

"On and off, four months. Whenever Simon's away I come. You'll get whiskey, you know, but he always gets me sherry."

"Why is that?"

"He likes what it does to my breath, he says. Actually he's a bit of a skinflint."

"Same old David."

"Really? What do you mean by that?"

But David came in just then with his drinks — two whiskeys in greasy-looking reclaimed peanut butter jars and a sherry for Margot in a shot glass. "This languid young waif is Margot, Mark. She's something of a fixture here, so she says, and in other flats as well."

"You're vile, David."

"Yes, vile. Move over." David grabbed two thickish

ankles as though they were edges of a newspaper full of dog-do, lifted them and sat down beside Margot. The ankles dropped back in his lap. "Don't you ever wash, woman?" he said, and without waiting to hear her answer turned to me and asked, "What've you been up to since we saw you last? Went home to America, killed off the wogs in Veet-nahm, now what?"

I told him I had taught school after the war.

"Still doing that?"

"No, I packed it in. Marjorie and I are living in New York."

"She's rich, I hear."

"Not really. Who told you that?"

"Well, we manage," he said. "I'm still poor, though. Haven't had good bourbon whiskey since we went down. Tell me about that fount of lucre you're married to. I've had good reports."

"Marjorie's fine. She sends love. Maybe you'll meet her this visit."

"When do you go back?"

"Late next week, I think."

"Mark has a super wife, Margot."

"How would you know? You've never met her."

"I have reports from trusted agents."

"What rot."

"Does your wife wash, Mark?"

"Perpetually."

"I wish you'd wash, Margot. Go have a wash."

"Later."

"Is your wife obedient, Mark."

"Alas, no."

"There, you see!" the girl said.

I somehow resented their intimacy. Later — I had

gone into the kitchen to get more liquor — I heard David go into the john off the hallway between the sitting room and pantry. He was still there when I walked back down the hall with the drinks. The bathroom door was ajar, enough for me to hear his slash and also to hear Margot talking to him inside while he peed. Presumably she was having a wash. And I thought, they aren't married but they use the bathroom at the same time. David could tell her to kiss off whenever he felt like it; they were thoroughly domesticated; he smelled her breath in the mornings when they woke up in their grubby bed, found her Kotexes when he emptied wastebaskets, endured her bitchiness.

But he could unload her. I resented it, or perhaps I should say — we were friends after all — I envied him.

We sat together again in the cold living room and I got David to talk. He launched into a long account of his medical training, a surprisingly spirited description of his classes and studies and ward duties which he told holding Margot's hand. She seemed proud of his achievement and from time to time looked sharply at me: I had left Cambridge with a good degree and a certain reputation for academic doggedness; now I was unemployed; David, whom she must have fancied I patronized in those days, had left the university with a miserable degree and was now a physician. She struck an attitude of satisfied primness.

The idea that David was serious about medicine, or committed to anything but his own pleasure, remained difficult to believe. I could think of him only as he had been at Cambridge, where his irreverence about his prospective profession had been notorious. And in a society in which medical humor had practically attained the status of an art form, he had managed to distinguish himself as the grossest premedical student anyone had ever known. In the college he had lived strictly to *épater le bourgeois:* to shock and buffet and offend the sensibilities of the community, particularly its senior members and the women unlucky enough to be around him. He was both elfin and hard-boiled. "Medicine is no joke," I told him once.

His answer was characteristic: "It's the greatest joke of all."

Among the more fiendish of David's stunts one lingers in the mind. It was executed on the night of the College's May Ball, when he was one of twenty guests invited to a stiffly elegant dinner beforehand in Grantchester. Hostesses had much trepidation about inviting him to dinners, but he had wrangled an invitation that night on promise of good behavior and had — at least through the drinks and first couple of courses — behaved himself. It was at about this time — I was sitting directly across from him at the table — that I noticed he was eating with his left hand only. I asked him why. He responded by putting his forefinger to his lips, enjoining my patience. I would see why soon enough.

David had spent most of the afternoon preparing one of the fingers of his right hand for service as a medical exhibit: it had been bathed in peroxide and iodine; a deep cleft had been gouged down the center of the fingernail, a slot which would anchor a thin piece of India-rubber which he wrapped around the top of the finger. Now it resembled a miniature German helmet. For good measure small fragments of the rubber, blackened in ink, had been attached about the first knuckle, just below the visor of the helmet, wart-like excrescences intended to approximate some sort of tropical or venereal fungus. Thus cosmeticized, the hideous shaft was now thrust through a hole at the narrow end of an ordinary match-box tray, bedded down on a couch of surgical gauze, and its lower half covered like a blanket with a Furacin pad.

"More wine, David?" Our hostess Lady Urfingham stood behind him.

"Thanks awfully," he answered. "And I should like you to meet the bishop." He had, as I say, kept his right hand in the pocket of his dinner jacket during the first part of the meal. Now, with a devilish child's smirk on his face, he pulled it out, removed the tray from its cover, and proceeded to introduce his hostess to the bishop, to what was a really creditable representation of a human penis recently separated from a cadaver.

Lady Urfingham blanched and fainted like a cadet in a summer parade. The bishop was returned immediately to his see, and thence to David's pocket, with the result that no one else saw him that evening, and that Lady Urfingham was thought to have had too much to drink.

Sometimes David's sense of fun got the better of him with more serious repercussions. On his final examinations, being asked "Fully to describe a piece of original clinical research undertaken during your term as an undergraduate member of this university," David offered the following:

Senecan haemaglobin Clog (Bell-ringer's syndrome): During the undergraduate tenure of the undersigned, research by the self-same clearly established that church-wardens who had died while in employ in Ely Cathedral — than which Earth hath not anything to shew more fair — had, in eight of eleven known cases, given up their souls as a result of prolonged exposure to the holocaustic cacophony of church-bells.

The examination answer continued in this wry vein for several pages of the bluebook, footnoted throughout with references to hitherto unknown scientists and diseases.

David was rusticated and made to take his examinations over again the following summer.

He had been talking for twenty minutes, and his face had taken on a strange umber coloration as the light drained from the room. There were sounds of congesting traffic from Bayswater Road and I began to think I should leave.

"It wasn't all serious, of course," he was saying. "I did a bit of interning at St. Thomas's two years ago. One of the requirements was that you assist in each of the twenty most common procedures."

I asked him which one he liked best.

"Live births, no question. My dolly was an Ahf-rikan lady who had already had eleven, so she said. The infant shot across the room like a purple torpedo. I had only to catch it."

"Did you?"

"Alas."

"And now you're a neurosurgeon."

"A neurosurgeon living, as we used to say, in sin. Margot, fetch us a dinner. Give her a couple of quid, old boy, she'll bring the food round."

I found some money and gave it to her. She bounded heavily down the stairs.

"What you think of her?"

"No opinion."

"I'm off for Liverpool late tonight or early tomorrow morning. Pay her a visit. She'll be here."

"For God's sake, David."

"Good Friend, for Christe's sake, forbear, eh?" He sat running his finger around the rim of the drinking jar, determinedly droll. It was almost as though we were back in our rooms at college, eight years ago, except that I had the sense he was disappointed in himself, as though he had planned to convince me that his work now absorbed him utterly. He rocked slowly back and forth on the edge of his sofa, saying nothing.

"What in God's name would I want to pay *her* a visit for?"

"Thought you had no opinion of her."

"I'm not turned on by her, if that's what you mean."

"Best kind in that case. Surely you fornicated with the wogs?"

"No, I never did. Really."

"I don't believe you."

"Believe anything you want."

"Blessed are the pure in spirit," he said.

"I'm married, David, remember?"

"She put you through hell eight years ago, remember?"

"That was eight years ago."

"Balls," he said.

"I'm happily married."

"Where's your wife?"

"In Lawnsmere with the children, either at the hotel or at her uncle's."

"Behaves herself, does she?"

For the first time since our marriage I wondered if she did. "Immaculate," I said.

"You think, ay?"

"I think."

"You know?"

"Somewhere in between."

"So come up tomorrow and see Margot. Tell your wife you're onto a relative of the man you're doing research about. Can only see him Sunday. Love to bring her with you but can't. Matters of great pith and moment." He brought his hands together and struck a prayerful pose, resting his front teeth on the tips of his forefingers.

"I'd better go, David."

"We've just ordered dinner, old boy."

"I really must."

"Back to your little love nest?"

"Perhaps I'll be back. Will Margot be here all day tomorrow?"

"She doesn't go to church."

"She'll be here then."

"Will if I tell her to."

"Tell her to, then, doctor. Have her eat my dinner too, put some beef on her."

"Plenty of that on her now. One could quibble about its distribution."

"I won't quibble."

"Good old Mark."

"Goodbye, David. See you next week, maybe. How long are you in Liverpool for?"

"Two days at the most. Probably back here tomorrow night or Monday. Christmastide, you know."

"Goodbye, David."

"*Hypocrite lecteur,*" he said, in throaty Parisian French. "*Hypocrite lecteur! Mon semblable! Mon frère!*"

27

That night I told Marjorie I had to go up to London in the morning. She was very tired and said only "OK" and flipped her book to the floor and went to sleep. She didn't say anything the next morning, either, except as we were finishing breakfast in our rooms. To this day I have no idea if she suspected me.

"Why're you going to London?"

"Interview a great-nephew of the general's."

"On Sunday?"

"Like most people he works the rest of the week. London isn't Far Hills."

"Giles said he never heard of Gordon Sandstone."

"Well?"

"You promised the children you'd take them to Sterrett Castle."

"You seen one castle you seen them all."

"They haven't *seen* one castle."

"I'll take them tomorrow or Tuesday."

"You won't take them. You know you won't."

"I said I would. If you don't believe me, have Orme take them."

"He hates children."

"Giles, then. How many times have you told me Giles was good with children?"

"Don't you love your own children?"

"I'm not going to be drawn, Marjorie."

"I want Uncle Frederick to take us," my daughter said. I picked her up and kissed her. "Uncle Frederick, ay? Who's Uncle Frederick?"

"Uncle Frederick Giles," her mother answered. "In the absence of her newly diligent father the only other American in the hotel is now 'uncle' to her."

"You like Uncle Frederick?"

"Uncle Frederick said baseball is dead," my daughter said, looking at Marjorie.

"In what context was this?"

"He's played ball with them in the garden every day you've been in London."

"Tell Uncle Frederick you want to use him for home plate."

"Mark!"

"He's been good to them, I know that. Don't stuff it down my throat. He's trying to impress you, so he's good to them."

My daughter's eyes darted from Marjorie to me and back to Marjorie like a spectator's at a tennis match. At six, her capacity to give pain was fully developed, and she knew her skill. She vaguely connected baseball with her father's pleasure. And as vaguely, perhaps, but with an instinct as deadly in its aim as it was accurate in its apprehension, she saw there was something in London I would rather do than take her to a castle. Also she understood that Marjorie perhaps did not believe my story about interviewing a relative of General Sandstone's. In fine, she knew better than Marjorie what was going on, and I noticed the tiniest quiver of malicious amusement in her lower lip and saw her huge gray eyes flick back to mine. At the same time — a beautifully patronizing gesture — she put her hand on my son's head and patted him.

"Alright," Marjorie said.

"You enjoy being with him, don't you?"

"Mark, get your coat and your bloody notebooks and get out of here. Go to London and interview your idiotic general's great-nephew."

"Are you going to get Giles to take you to Sterrett Castle?"

"Maybe." Now my daughter vaulted onto her lap, and she leaned back against Marjorie and rubbed the back of her head against her mother's cheek and looked at me evenly, but again with that wry quiver at her lips. "Or maybe we'll go out to Orme's for the day. Whichever, I'll decide after you leave."

So I left, figuring they'd go out to Orme's, and when I turned at the door to wave I saw my son was sitting at Marjorie's feet, leaning against her chair, and that the three of them were staring at me together. They regarded me — I can only say — clinically, but with a certain detached amusement that made me shudder.

"Have a good time, Daddy," my son said, speaking for them all.

28

A bluefly was trapped between the shade and the window of David's tiny bedroom. "Kill that son of a bitch, Margot," I said to her. She went over to the window and scrunched the thing between the shade and the window like a piece of popcorn. It dropped drily to the window sill.

"It was a wasp," she said, walking back to the bed. The mattress gave thickly with the weight of her sitting astride my buttocks. She poured a cold pool of alcohol between my shoulder blades and caught its running down my spine with the heel of her hand. Had it run farther down my spine it would have burnt her horribly, an interesting notion, though I had no wish to hurt her.

"A wasp?" In my daydreams I had imagined I would commit adultery for the first time in the afternoon, on some hot airless afternoon in the bleak and dusty room near a bus station. The windows of the room would have no curtains and the shades would be yellowed. David's room was enough like it to make the frieze recognizable. I could hear Margot swallowing and also, from time to time, there was a raspy interior grating at the radiator.

"Do you like that?" she said.

"Those are my love handles you're flabbing."

"Love handles? Is that what they're called in America?"

She began rubbing wetly at the nape of my neck. I

remembered at that time, God knows why, that when I had sat on a court-martial board trying a private first class for sodomy, another member of the board had slid the Manual for Courts-Martial in front of me and had underlined the appropriate provision: *penetration, however slight, is sufficient to complete the act.*

Now this was wonderful, no? If you kept your tongue in your mouth you should be within your rights. Otherwise there must be trouble. A bare millimeter of thrust and you were *de jure* a sodomite, or an adulterer even, depending on the circumstances of the case. Twice damned then, tried, convicted, trussed, hung, drawn, quartered: your privy parts fed to mongrel dogs before your eyes, while the authorities staunched the bloodspurt with dung. The punishment was now less barbarous, but the language of the provision remained adamant. We are not amused, it said. Senator Thurmond was not amused by the Pentagon Papers, but John Kenneth Galbraith was amused. They were such a bore! he thought. No, the authorities are not amused. Every eventuality must be provided for. Whosoever were to take any carnal member and/or members into any orifice/s of his or her body whatsoever shall be adjudged to have completed the act. Do we make ourselves clear? A plea of *coitus interruptus* would not be accepted in extenuation. The statute was mute as to the site of ejaculation; and the Army was particular as to orifices only if said orifices into which the carnal members had penetrated were orifices for which the aforementioned members had not by nature been intended.

As I say, precision in the wording of the statute was demanded by the severity of the charges brought against those accused. *This is not funny, Lieutenant Adams, and*

I conjure you not to laugh. I wanted to laugh harder, but did not. "Sir."

Private Ripples, nineteen, banal, and married, had put his carnal member into a collie dog.

"How *old* was the animal?" Colonel Fairbrooke demanded.

"Thirteen, sir."

"Thirteen! Months or years, lad?"

"Thirteen years old, sir."

"Dog or bitch, lad?"

"Dog, sir."

"Why'd you do it, son?"

"Don't know, colonel. Just did it."

Fairbrooke's eyes were ice blue, and his Lectric-shaved pate shone. His Board could convict Ripples for sodomy, adultery, and homosexuality — all at once, he must have been thinking. He gnawed at his pencil and looked abstractedly at the magnificent MP standing behind the accused. With all the myrmadoon sheep and nubile young cockers running around Fort Hall, with all the colonels' daughters and waitresses and civil servant secretaries and teaching apprentices and thick Sunnybrook Farm types in eastern Dakota — with all these, Private Ripples had elected to place his carnal member in a collie dog of advanced age. There had been penetration, certainly. Ripples, toeing at the floor in front of the table like an athlete accepting a trophy, had willingly admitted it. He knew his rights. The hell with them. He done it, he said.

"Jesus, Adams," Fairbrooke whispered. I was sitting at his immediate left on the side of the table nearest the wall. Behind and below us in the street a platoon of recruits sounded delayed cadence. Above us there was hung a picture of Washington, the picture with the strato-nimbus-whatever clouds at the leader's breast. Private Ripples had three alternatives as he stood before the silent deliberative Board: he could stare down at his boots as they toed away, wondering if their absurd spit shine would get him off; he could look at Washington — a distinctly unappetizing prospect for a sodomite, I should have thought; or he could look at us members of the Board. He chose the last, and he looked at me because he had heard me repress a snicker. I smirked at him. "Jesus, Adams, it's no joke what this kid's done." Colonel Fairbrooke whispered well; Ripples could not hear him.

"I know it, sir," I whispered back. "It's heinous and ghastly." Fairbrooke and I, by the way, attended Divine Service together each Sunday in the Episcopal Chapel.

"You may go, lad, you may go. Take him out of here."

A majority of the officers present concurring, Ripples was incarcerated in the Fort Hall stockade, it being further stipulated that no books, magazines, or other printed matter, cartoon, caricature, pasquinade or picture which might be construed as making primary appeal to the prurient interests of the service member be furnished said member for the period of his forthcoming incarceration. We could not tolerate sodomites among us, that much was sure, though I suggested a more fitting punishment might have been a jail-sentence *with* access to the naughty literature.

I chuckled, remembering it.
"How old are you, Margot?"

"Why do you ahsk?"

"I don't know. Just curious."

"I'm making curlicues with the alcohol on your latissimus dorsi. David teaches me medical words. Can you feel the curlicues?"

"Is the Pope a Catholic?"

"And now I must go lower."

"Indeed you must, madam."

She hunkered backward, gripping down along my thighs and calves. Now she sat on my ankles. I felt her tug at my underpants until they were down over the backs of my knees.

"Do my buttocks."

"Your bottom?"

"You know."

"Your gluteus maximus."

"That's it."

"A quite pleasant bottom it is, too. Perhaps muscular once, now fallen away in the fullness of time."

I lay the side of my head on the backs of my hands and looked around at her, watching her eyes. She seemed quite absorbed in her work.

"You wish to copulate, don't you?"

"Clever woman."

"I can see you wish to copulate. Turn over. We shall do that, and more, my dear Mark."

She was so formal, and her technique so ritualized, that I had a momentary vision of liveried servants in Zouave trousers fanning us; I could almost hear the players of a small orchestra saluting us with a concerto grosso from outside our *chambre d'amour*.

De jure I was a sodomite. Margot was splendidly ardent but her ministrations bore the stamp of much practice. Meantime another wasp went to buzzing between the window and the shade; Margot disengaged herself with an affecting reluctance. "Shall I kill that son of a bitch?"

"Kill him."

I watched her walk towards the window again and was disappointed in the thickness of her waist. She despatched the wasp with the back of her fist in a triumphant girlish gesture which made her right breast, outlined against the smoky tan shade, flounce and stand out. "You gross man," she said, walking back.

"Back to your work, Margot."

"Back to my work." As she came back I noticed her cheeks were slack and waffling like an epileptic's. Now she knelt on the floor and put her arms under me as though she were going to lift me like a child, and again she went down to her task, more heartily than before, returning to an abandoned pleasure with much joy in it. I motioned for her to swing up onto the bed, to swing over me. Twice sodomized, I was. Since it was now four o'clock in London, it would be ten at Fort Hall, and perhaps Colonel Fairbrooke in his dress blues would be striding down the aisle to his pew in Chapel. However slightly, I thought of this individual, this excellent soldier, and I decided to buy the latest *Penthouse* before leaving for Lawnsmere.

"*I'm no good this way,*" Margot said suddenly, words that excited me wildly.

It was over as quickly as I realized how much I wanted to be away from her.

"That was very smooth," she said. "Very efficient. Nasty, brutish and short, just as I like it."

What the hell did she mean by that? I didn't ask her. Instead I asked her if this was how David liked it.

"Oh, yes, he's not particular. Is your wife beautiful? David says she is."

"Yes, very beautiful."

"And rich?"

"Yes, richer than a queen. Gowns of purple and lemon-gold and creamy-white hang in her closets. Vast jewels, diamonds and peridots, *topazes de fuego*, garnets and sapphires. And hundreds of unguents at her dressing table. The lawns of her father's house are shaved by men in business suits."

"Has she on those Gucci shoes when she goes out?"

"Always. She wears them in bed, even."

"You have children, don't you?"

"Yes, three children. I am known to have sired at least three children."

"All at Lawnsmere with you?"

"No, we only brought two with us."

"Got a fag?"

I gave her the pack off the bedtable. "David likes these. I used to get them for him when we were at Cambridge."

"You shared your cigarettes there, too, and your women?"

"That is very true."

"What sort of women were they?"

"Bluestockings and goody-goodies. The former stank; the latter . . ."

"The latter masturbated with peppermint sticks . . ."

"Nice way to talk. What time is it, Margot?"

"Half-five."

"I've got to go."

"First you come, then you go."

"That's not very funny," I said. I finished dressing, and remembered to pick up my notebooks in the living room.

"You've a train to catch?"

"Trains to catch and promises to keep." I splayed her a kiss from my fingertips and bowed my way backwards out of the room, like a colonel leaving a queen his royal mistress. But she seemed not to notice, sitting there on the side of the bed, one leg jacknifed onto the other, picking at her big toe.

29

Tomorrow was December 24th, the day on which we were to have stuffed ourselves into one of those tightly sprung, jouncing, vomity English rent-a-cars and driven with the children to Cambridge to hear and watch the Ceremony of Lessons and Carols at King's; then to have taken lodging for the night in some remote Essex village in a snug close inn; then to have made honest uninnovative love in an oak-framed bed under a scarlet canopy and an eiderdown; then to have returned Christmas Day to Lawnsmere, driving through a delicate snow shower with a love child quickening in Marjorie's womb. Wasn't this why we had come over in the first place?

It was partly true. It was also the argument I used on Marjorie that night sometime after returning from Margot and David's, coming down hard on her on the assumption that your fledgling adulterer might arouse suspicions in his wife by seeming preoccupied, ruminative — by being taciturn. I would be well advised to be my ordinary self. Under the circumstances it wasn't difficult.

In fact I did want to go to Cambridge. Coming back from London on the train I remembered a party we'd gone to in New York some months before, a party at which, very late, the host had played a wobbling old record of the Ceremony of Lessons and Carols: of the unforced, slightly sharp, chiming sounds of the boys: the "Sussex Carol," "Once in Royal David's City"; of their descanted "*Adeste Fideles*"; of the interposed voices of finely aged deacons and deans and young acolytes reading from scripture; and of the bishop intoning the blessing and his supplication for unity and brotherhood over all the earth, but especially in Her Majesty's dough-minions, and for those who mourn, for the lit-tle children, and for those who know not the Lord Jesus.

Her Majesty's pissy-assed dominions, said our cynical host, sickened by the "sentimentality" of the ceremony and watching tears well up in his wife's eyes. "Fucking Gibraltar and Jamaica and the Isle of Man, where manx cats come from. Her Majesty's goddamned dominions. What the hell kind of acoustics they got in that chapel, anyway?" That morning the Prince of Wales had made a parachute jump into the Channel and half the British Navy had stood by to pick him up. "Shouldda let the little bastard drown."

"People like you ought to drown," I told him. That night in the cab we decided to go to England.

But now Marjorie was insisting we stay in Lawnsmere and have our Christmas Eve at Orme's party; that was where we belonged, and what the children deserved, and they wouldn't get in his way; and besides, we had made friends in the Rufus Arms and in Lawnsmere — or she had, at least.

"Frederick Giles?"

"Alright, Frederick Giles. At least he's not Byzantine like you."

"Byzantine? You buy a thesaurus at the chemist's?"

"Mark."

"Stay away from him, will you?"

"Please?" she said, ignoring me. "We can't drive all the way to Cambridge tomorrow, not with the children."

"Leave them with Mrs. Nance."

"On Christmas Eve?"

"Why not? We could get back here by two or three."

"No," she said, "I won't go."

I gave in to her as I had planned to, wondering if I was giving myself away in doing it. We would stay in Lawnsmere and see Orme.

He was Marjorie's uncle on her mother's side. He had come home to Greylarch on Friday; Marjorie and the children had spent Saturday afternoon and most of today with him — Giles, it turned out, having gone off on a short tour in the west of England.

We should be bloody fools, Orme had said to us on a visit to America more than a year ago, if we did not stay in Lawnsmere. It was easy to gauge what freight the "bloody fool" was meant to bear: he wanted us with him, he was genuinely fond of us, but he wanted us to stay in Lawnsmere and not at his estate. Commodious as it was, it would not suit our children properly, if we caught his drift. He winked, something not many Englishmen do, letting us know that though he wanted us near him, we must not be offended by his well-known aversion to children, particularly children who poured Dr Pepper on his British warm, children who told him when he foolishly had dandled them on his knee that his breath smelt funny.

Orme Goderich was a singular man. He was very "fit," having never smoked or drunk anything stronger than wine — of which, however, he was a great connoisseur — and having retained his boyish fondness for cold showers three times a day. His life was ordered as if by a metronome; variations in its pace unsettled him. He was immaculately clothed and insisted on right angles and perfect alignments. He laughed at himself often and took snuff off his left forefinger.

Orme's political hero was George Canning, whom he called the author of the Mon-roe Doctrine. He liked to quote him, and his favorite Canning *mot* was this: "I have no use for Areopagus and the like of that." I later discovered this meant that neither Orme nor Canning could stand old men in government, and that Orme's great enemy, the Ministry of Defence in London, was full of them: the Ministry, as he said, with its quibbling old men, its feckless culture of the memorandum and its moral eunuchs and its grubby little leftishists who had dogged him all through his distinguished but abbreviated military career — from which he had been placed on the retired list as Colonel Orme Goderich, MC, OBE, as recently as 1967. He was then forty-nine. The year before that the Ministry had ordered him to duty in London, among themselves. Orme had refused the orders, had thrown over what must have been a reasonable chance of being promoted brigadier, and had demahnded and gowt diuty as Inspector, Territorial and Reserve Forces, Mid-Surrey.

This had of course been a sinecure, but that was bloody well alright. One nipped in for a look at the St. Neot's cadet corps, did a bit of speaking and recruiting, and saw to it that the reserve matériel was kept up: dinky-toy armored cars, Sten guns without firing pins, wastebaskets, the men's kit. For the rest, he was at leisure to enjoy what he still called the loveliest of England's counties, and his own considerable property in it — some 290 acres of tangled copse, groves of poplar and cedar, and fragrant rolling meadowland cross-sected by clear brooks and bordered at its northern limit by the Spley.

Greylarch, his house, would bear visiting, he said. Orme doubted Marjorie remembered it too well after all her years in America — she was too dam-nably beautiful to have a memory; yet he fancied she could attest that it was sturdy and warm; that it had a cellar full of "cynical" wines, jouvet sauternes and cabernet sauvignons of distinguished lineage, and plenty of high-stomached port. Or perhaps she had been too young to taste of them — no matter, no matter. But there was his library of the great war which I must rummage about in, the war in which Buonaparte (he pronounced it Bwon-ah-partay) and the Frogs had been sent packing. He would not pollute the conversation with further references to that morally unclassifiable being. There were horses as powerful as Vergil's and sleek as the Godolphin barb. There was fishing in his streams and croquet and bowls on his lawns and no bloody telephones, except at his steward's, to ruin one's leisure.

No doubt of it, he had said, his arm avuncularly about Marjorie's waist: we must not come to England without a visit to Lawnsmere. And he trusted that would be soon. The three of us stood at the edge of the soccer-field at Grierson and watched a fiery autumn sunset which silhouetted a lower-school intramural game. I noticed how much the soccer pleased him and I was grateful that he had seen a boys' school. He had spent almost three weeks touring in the United States, but by his own account had seen only the Liberty Bell, the River Rouge Car Factory, Disneyland, Cape Kennedy and New York City. He fancied he knew our country now.

And remembering all of this, but especially the goodness, the vitality and frankness of Orme, and hearing Marjorie's excited shout that the Ceremony of Lessons and Carols was to be televised in any case, and thinking that Orme would probably put on a pretty fair Christmas Eve party, I reconciled myself to Christmas Eve at Greylarch.

Post coitum naughty animal shaky est. In the hour and a half that had elapsed between my return from Margot's and Marjorie's arrival from Orme's I had sat in the pub at the Rufus reading my silly *Penthouse* magazine. I was alone, except for Carstairs — who appeared to be doing some sort of mechanical work on the cash register behind the bar: who, from time to time, would look at me over his steel half-rims as if mildly insulted that I wasn't sitting at the bar talking to him.

"Where's my countryman?" I finally asked.

"Gone to the West. Back tomorrow. Gone to look at Winchester and Wells."

"Good riddance, I guess."

Carstairs said nothing but smiled faintly, like a woman admitting to a friend's indiscretion. He slammed the drawer of the cash register shut and disappeared into the pantry. A minute or two later he was sitting next to me.

"Don't like that chap, do you?"

"Should I like him?"

"Why shouldn't you? You know, Mr. Adams, first impressions are often wrong impressions. Not saying you should like him, of course, but you've only had drinks with him once or twice. Lots of good men shoot their mouths off at night." He looked at me owlishly, as though he had just put my king in check.

"I'll be frank with you, Mr. Carstairs," I said, "I think he's a little sweet on my wife. I also happen to think he's an ass, and that clods like him give my country a bad name abroad."

"You do, do you?"

"Yes."

"Well, it happens you may be right. But we've got used to him here, Mr. Adams. Eight or ten times he's stayed here, he has. He's beastly to most everyone. Never quite bad enough for us to fling him out on his ear, but damn near. But there's no malice in him, I don't think."

"Has he behaved himself around Marjorie?"

"Oh, I think so. Has a bit of a flirt with her, you know. She doesn't seem to mind. He's very good with your children and you're not around much during the day. Are you, now?" He spoke as if perhaps he sensed I was having a bit of a flirt myself, up in London. He went on: "Mr. Giles's been through a lot, you know. I should imagine he's told your wife. His first wife burnt to death in a fire in Chicago two days before the Germans captured him. Then he had cancer five or six years ago. He's a lonely man."

"What kind of cancer?"

"Skin, I think, something to do with his skin."

"What do they do when I'm in London?"

"Shouldn't worry if I were you. They've gone on walks and drives, played cards in the reading room. Of course your wife was with Colonel Goderich most of today."

"My children always around?"

"You *are* worried, aren't you?"

"Are they? When Giles and Marjorie are together?"

"Usually," he said calmly. "Deirdre looked after them one afternoon, took them for a walk round the town — Thursday I think. They're beautiful children. I should keep an eye on them, if I were you."

"The children or Giles and Marjorie?"

"Well," he paused, judging the proper limit of discretion, "All of them I suppose. But you've nothing to worry about, I don't think."

"You're damn right I don't. Marjorie interested in that loudmouth? Never. You ever listen to his spiels in here?"

"Many times, sir, many times."

"Well?"

"Quite right. Quite right."

Looking at Carstairs I thought of that line from "Prufrock": ". . . deferential, glad to be of use, full of high sentence, but a bit obtuse," whatever it was. The hotel keeper had moved with accomplished ease from the role he appeared to covet, that of confidante, to the other role for which he was so well fitted — the efficient, accommodating giver of goods and services.

I did not know him well, and it did not occur to me until months later, when we were back in New York, that Carstairs was Giles's friend, that he would be among the last to speak ill of him in anything but unessentials. I thought him a good judge of people then, as I still do; but, making the easy assumption that the Rufus Arms boarded Giles only because he stayed in an expensive suite and spent freely at the bar, and knowing that Carstairs decided who stayed in the hotel, I had calculated that he found Giles as obnoxious as we did.

As *we* did? I still couldn't imagine Marjorie being seriously attracted to Giles. I couldn't imagine him daring to make a pass at her. I sat there with my drink and thought of Dan Dunphy — the old boxing announcer — describing what I'd do to him if he did: *a leftanaright to th' head, annanother left to the chest, and a solid uppercut to the jaw anna smashing right to the belly.* A surging, upward-seeking right to the stomach, to Giles's flat but probably soft stomach. My knuckles would be bruised by the ventral jagged ladder of his spine, and he would turn away to vomit; and seizing his head I would thrust and press him to the floor, rubbing his face against the grain of the splintering wood, disfiguring and maiming him irretrievably. As for Marjorie: I did not think I would divorce her; there was too much mileage to be unrolled out of such an incident for that. No. Perhaps I would take the children from her and hide with them somewhere until that inevitable time she should come begging and whimpering back to us.

"I say, you are wrought up, aren't you?"

"Has he ever made a pass at women staying in the hotel?"

"Haggish widows. No one like your wife."

"Any luck?"

He pursed his lips and gave an accommodating, curt little nod: "I should have thought so. Lot of women'll sleep with anything. So will a lot of men."

"Has he made a pass at your daughter?"

"Deirdre hates him."

"Susan?"

"No. He's a snob about the help."

"Never gone after either of them, then?"

"I shouldn't have thought so."

The language of discretion. *Should have thought. Shouldn't have thought. On balance it would appear. One might suppose. One wonders. On the other hand.* A certain quality of tentativeness in all matters is England's most distinguishing national characteristic.

Just then four young men in pouchy sweaters came into the pub and walked to the bar. Carstairs excused himself to serve them. "See for yourself tomorrow night," he said.

"Tomorrow night? . . ."

"Your wife asked us all to Colonel Goderich's party."

"Him too?"

"Him too."

Giles too. Soon afterwards Marjorie came in with the children and we had our little set-to. I played contrary with her, as you have seen, and I did not mention her inviting Giles to Goderich's party. I would let her have a certain amount of rope, but I would keep the end of it in my own hands, deciding what to do with it; and, indeed, wondering if I'd have to do *anything* with it. The whole thing was preposterous.

30

"What time we due at Orme's?"

"Nine," Marjorie said.

"Shall I fetch Lover Boy?"

"You do that, Big One. But please . . ."

But I closed the door on Marjorie and headed off to Giles's room. We had not seen him, but he had been due back that day, December 24th, at six.

Marjorie and I had had a pleasant day, reader, a kind of remission in the form of a flying visit to London without the children. There were no enervating side effects as yet.

We had had fun in London — of a certain furtive and determined sort. We had looked in at Apsley House, once the home of the greatest Frog-hater of them all; walked between long lines of hanging body armor at the Wallace Collection; had a thick aleish lunch at Simpson's; bought toys for the children in Burlington Arcade; seen the Gurkhas relieve the Welsh Guards in front of the "Buckhouse"; and come at last to a dark haven in a movie house off Leicester Square.

I remember reading somewhere in the reminiscent works of that excellent intellectual Edmund Wilson that he too had once entered a flickhouse for similar purposes — on 42nd Street in Manhattan during the coronary hours of a raw winter afternoon. He wanted only to rest, having felt a sniggering anginal whisper in his chest, and had doddered into the theater, not looking at the screen until he had found himself a seat. Then he had arranged himself comfortably, had disencumbered himself of his galoshes and gloves and settled back for some diverting amusement. Finally he had looked towards the screen, hitched up his glasses and seen: "A human vagina, some fifteen feet high." In the memoir he described the prospect in a marvelous kind of field-manual deadpan.

The English projectionist offered us an opening prospect not dissimilar to the object of Mr. Wilson's shocked attention — with the exception that ours was, as it were, in violent throbbing use. Its owner had squatted down like an inverted slingshot over the loin and shaft of a scrawny youth who lay on a shag-carpeted floor with his forearm over his eyes. The couple had enormous staying power ("That's what they're paid for, don't forget that," Marjorie whispered); and no intensity of effort, however redoubled or redirected, seemed to avail them. The breathing of the youth became stertorous and rasping and finally, I thought, even desperate: it was as though he was trying to breathe through a gas mask. The woman bounced and flopped about on him — really, she seemed to be a good sport about it — and on and on they went.

But suddenly the young man barked out the word "Love!" and then, more tenderly, " 'E love yer," and his exhausted partner fell forward and buried her face in his neck. " 'E love yer, lad," she said.

"Do you love me, Marjorie?"

"I love ya, dearie," she said.

"But this is so filthy, this business on the screen. I've got half a mind to speak to the management."

"It *is* filthy. To think it could happen in Wordsworth's own country!"

"Eh?"

"It's reprehensible."

"But we should give it another forty or fifty minutes. We musn't indict the whole film on what may be an isolated lapse of taste."

"You're right, Mark, dead right."

So we sat watching for another half hour or so, and confined ourselves to polite expressions of disbelief and admiration for the imperturbability of the players; and finally to a whispered agreement that nothing in the film seemed to endow it with any redeeming social value, and that it was therefore our duty as citizens of the Anglo-American community to remove ourselves from the theater at once, and as noisily as possible.

"You wish to make a scene, then," Marjorie said.

We chose our moment carefully, waiting patiently for the projection of an unnatural act — which was not long in coming. Marjorie began with a display reminiscent of her performance many years ago at Tanglewood, hurling her newspaper to the floor, jumping up from her seat as if sprung from a trampoline, and filling the narrow theater with an outraged, sibilant "Dis-gusting! This is sodomy! Shame, Shame!" We ran up the aisle together, Marjorie threatening the viewers with my umbrella. "This kind of filth in England?" she screamed. "Has Prince Philip seen this? And the Crown Prince?" And so on, out into the street.

We kept up the charade for the rest of the afternoon;

and on the way back to Lawnsmere we bought Batman comic books at Waterloo Station and made a great show of reading them aloud on the train. We assembled children's toys in the diningcar and set several wind-up soldiers loose in the aisle. We even placed one of those little laughboxes outside the door of the ladies' john — and were rewarded by a sudden metallic clattering within and the precipitate emergence of a horsey suburban matron who looked so fierce I could hardly help going up to ask her if anything were the matter. But everything was quite alright with her, thengkiew.

So we had been naughty little children that afternoon. It was as though we were trying to undo or efface the memory of everything that had happened to our marriage since Fort Hall; but that, knowing we could no more do this than undo the events of our marriage themselves, we had agreed to behave as we had once done together. Forgive me if I quote Giles's second favorite author: But It Was No Good.

Marjorie had just begun dressing the children when I left her to get Giles. Neither of us had mentioned him all that day, and silence, Marjorie must have thought, implied my acquiescence in her friendship — or whatever — with him. My small outrage at his being included in the evening's party had yielded quickly to annoyance and curiosity, a kind of malicious curiosity, I must admit: not only about how Goderich and his friends would judge Giles, but also, and mainly, about what he and Marjorie might do together in a situation like this.

What indeed did she make of him? In the light of what did happen later it is terribly difficult to imagine, to reconstruct or rather unravel her impulses and emotions at that time. I knew Marjorie then to be a woman of as complete independence of judgment as anyone I have ever met. I knew she was governed by her impulses, and that the only thing I could ever safely predict about her was that she would act unpredictably. I knew she was full of compassion for those she imagined wronged by society or misused by its self-appointed arbiters, and that she had probably come to regard ours as a marriage of convenience — however determined she might be to canter along in its loosening harness. I knew she considered me derelict as a father, indifferent as a lover, and, as she often said, a "cruel, cruel man," just now a man whose cruelty seemed to manifest itself in the contemptible badgering of a Midwestern nobody. "You give out contempt for him like a body smell, even when you're not talking to him," she said.

This must have counted most with her. And somehow, in ways at which I could only guess, Frederick Giles lured and attracted her: partly, I suppose, because she could use him as a weapon — she had done this before, of course — but also because he radiated some mysterious allure that those on whom it did not work could not understand; some appeal rooted in his contrariness, his seeming certainty about himself, who he was, where he belonged.

But I was now gripped by the sense that I was the one being used and wronged, and as before I felt myself partly indemnified by this sense. At the same time I still mustered enough detachment to watch them as a disinterested spectator as well a disconsolate and rueful — and guilty — principal.

31

Giles's door was cracked an inch or two. I let myself in and could tell from the tobacco smell he was around somewhere or had just stepped out. For a moment it was silent; then I heard spongy lapping noises from the bathroom and in their midst Giles's hearty greeting: "That you, Adams?"

"Porfirio Rubirosa."

"With his twenty-six-inch wong."

"Right. I'm reeling it in from the hallway right now."

"Ha-ha," he chortled. "Be out'na minute." I heard a sucking sound as he got out of the bathtub and the draining whoosh of water in the hotel's old plumbing. Then — a very nice touch indeed — the metal click of lock being fastened at the bathroom door. It made me remember a woman I'd sat behind in church many years ago. I had gotten to the service during the first hymn and slipped in behind her as she stood singing. Seeing me come in she reached down and picked her purse off the cushion in her pew; then she tucked it under her arm and went on singing.

I didn't say anything, though I imagine Giles expected me to. "Serious business underway in here, got me?" he shouted.

"OK," I said. "Have at it."

"Turn on the radio, Adams. Let's hear some sounds of Christmas. You'll have to fool with the dial. It's a clock job and I leave it turned to no station at all and turn the volume way up. The thing comes on in the morning and you think you're in hell. It always wakes you up."

You can imagine how curious I was about his room and things. While he sat in the bathroom I had two or three minutes to look at them.

His bed–sitting room was somewhat larger than our own, and much more tidy — Giles had the natural older bachelor's finickiness. To the left as you entered sat a plain black table. On it lay a blotter and a stack of paperback books. There was also a malachite vase shaped like a kylix. Straight ahead was the room's only window, the oriel window he had mentioned earlier, and like ours, it overlooked the High Street. Off to the right, its headboard against the wall that separated it from the bathroom, was a lumpy narrow bed with a pink bedspread; and against the wall — to the immediate right — a large wardrobe of oak contained Giles's clothes. There was also an easy chair, a kind of Barcalounger covered in chintz, and a luggage rack. By the head of the bed was a double-nozzled glass sink with a glass shelf over it. Giles had fitted some sort of device to the two nozzles, a green double-hosed contraption that mixed the hot and cold water.

The books were obviously Giles's, not the hotel's. Their titles were of interest in the light of an earlier conversation: *None Dare Call It Treason*; a *Collected Articles* of Mr. Ernie Pyle; *The War Poetry of K. R. Ritter-Hausen*; a Bible; *The Tyranny of the Male Orgasm*, by Jay Windham, "Ph.D."; a perfectly virgin copy, Mentor edition, of Ivan Goncharov's *Oblomov* — described on its back cover as a "book about a man who tries to get out of bed for five hundred pages"; and finally Field Marshall Lord Wavell's *Other Men's Flowers*. All these books but the

Bible had F. GILES written on the page edges, in the unmistakable eggshell-blue of a Flair pen.

Under these neatly stacked volumes lay several magazines: *Encounter, Playboy,* "A Tourist's Guide to Winchester Cathedral," and a dog-eared, greasy copy — probably left behind by an earlier tenant — of "All Together Now, Row!" It was a coach's manual for the training of eight-oared crews.

Three-by-five cards stuck out of the books, and certain passages in them had been underlined.

"Help yourself to anything you want, old buddy!"

"Everything going according to schedule in there?"

"Ha-ha, that's the stuff!"

"I'll get a glass of water."

The glass shelf over the sink actually sagged under its burden of pills and unguents: Braggi and Kanøn products, including tubes of skin-bronzer and premoisteners and a deodorant FOR USE ANYWHERE; a slim jar of Grecian Formula 16; bottles of Listerine and Bactriol. There were also: a brush set with sterling silver handles; two different toothpastes — one to protect, the other to brighten their owner's teeth; a box of Compoze and a little glass vial of Valium; Ben-Gay; and a jar of translucent little marbles which must have been vitamin E or wheat germ oil. The tumbler I drank from was one of those foldout models you take to camp.

Sitting on the edge of the bed I could see most of the contents of the wardrobe. There were the well-known smoking jacket and two suits, one of them a double-knit. The other, a blue pin-stripe, rather boxy-looking like those politicians wear, featured a perfectly symmetrical pocket hanky which, by lifting it up, I found to be no hanky at all — only, as its cardboard base advertised, a "Half-a-Hank."

Giles's pocket-baggage, laid out on the shelf of the wardrobe door, would have done credit to King Farouk: a box of Dunhills; several credit cards; the enameled flag of Our Country; a Seiko watch with a calendar affixed to the strap; a small plastic pocket receptacle stuffed full of pens, including both a BIC Banana and a Mont Blanc; dark glasses like those affected by pilots of the Strategic Air Command; a folded tuition bill from Culver Military Academy, payable for services provided F. Giles III; a pocket guide to dynamic tension; and, finally, I kid you not, a Grip-Tite prophylactic. An open pocket notebook displayed the names of several women in London, as well as the following entries, written in a crabbed but even hand:

> *arriviste:* one lately arrived; parvenu
> *anent,* prep: as regards, concerning
> *metamorphosis,* n: transfiguration.

Hanging from the other wardrobe door was a red-handled pectoral muscle developer.

The toilet was flushed and a moment later Giles appeared. By then I had leaned back on the bed and was reading a newspaper.

"Well, sir!" he said. He shook my hand vigorously, putting his left hand on my right forearm. "It's damn good to see you."

"How was your trip?"

Giles worked a towel tip in one of his ears and sat down by his table. The trip was fine, he said, very enlightening. He particularly admired Salisbury Cathedral. One guy built it, so it wasn't any hodgepodge of different styles. It had "organic cohesiveness."

On the other hand Gloucester Cathedral had not been worth a shit, in his opinion. He asked me if I'd ever heard the funny story about it, involving an American who had coughed up several hundred grand to help refurbish it. This American for some reason had to stay home in Texas when they dedicated the rebuilt part, so they sent him a tape recording of the dedicatory prayer, in which the artless bishop had wound up asking the worshipers to join him in thanking God for "this timely succor."

"Sucker — get it?"

That was rich. I asked him if he'd been to Winchester or Glastonbury.

"Not Glastonbury," he said, as if the question disappointed him. "That's not even a cathedral. For a church to be a cathedral, it has to be where the bishop is. Yeah, I spent a couple hours in Winchester, including going through that incredible school they have there, goddamned kids reading David Hume, crap like that. They probably can't add six and ten."

What else had he done?

"Emptied a little dirty water, Adams. Lawnsmere's not so hot for that."

"It's not, huh?"

"No, it's not." His voice remained even, bantering in tone. If he knew what I was asking, he showed utterly no sign of it.

"What I had out there was nothing to write home about, either."

"Too bad."

"You're lucky being married, living with your wife."

"I suppose I am."

"No, you are, you are." He stood up and began combing his hair. "What about this party tonight? What's this Goderich like? Lotta people be there?"

I told him I thought about forty or fifty and that I'd heard the party was an annual thing. I told him also — I could play his devious game — that Orme Goderich was his kind of man: a prodigious reader, very cultivated, good war record, Tory; but Giles answered only, "Yeah?" abstractedly.

"He's Marjorie's uncle, and very fond of her."

"Zegotny money?"

"Pretty well off."

He laid his comb on the shelf and began spraying his hair, lifting a clutch of hair at the back, spraying its underside and patting it in place over the bald spot. It reminded me a little of Marjorie ratting her hair.

Then he unscrewed a bottle, shook it until several pills had fallen out, put them on his tongue and jerked his head back. "Vitamin E, Adams. You know what they're good for, don't you?" He walked over to his wardrobe and began rummaging through the ties that hung there.

"How about a stinking foulard necktie?" I suggested.

He took it in good humor. "Nah, they're not me. I don't even own any."

"You're right," I said. "They're not you."

Later I wondered why I had said that, or rather, why I had engaged him so clumsily. We seemed almost like careful boxers circling around each other after meeting in the center of the ring for our instructions: boxers who had an odd respect for each other, who had perhaps even said "good luck" before we went at it. And yet I knew one of us had to put out a feeler, had to engage the other, and my remark, unbidden as it had come from my lips, was only an expected, flickering jab to Giles.

Yet it seemed to freeze him, if only for a second. He turned to face me, and with a look of sobering, fierce intensity he answered: "You don't like me, do you, Adams?"

"What makes you say that?"

"Think I'm blind? Turn the goddamn radio down."

He paused while I stretched around to turn the knob over his bed.

"Let me tell you a thing or two, young man. I can tell you don't like me. I could care less. I'll tell you something else: You don't like your wife either — if you ever did — or people. People in general."

"Why should I like you? Why should anyone like you, the way you act?"

He hid whatever anger this evoked. "Let me hit the ball back in your court. What do you find objectionable in me?" He turned around again, and now he leaned close to the mirror and pinched at the openings of his nostrils with his thumb and forefinger.

"I mean," he continued, "perhaps we can exorcise those demons of hatred and arrogance that pollute the waters of your character."

Did he use language like this because its euphemisms distanced him from the ugliness of what he had to say? Did he know how ridiculous, how asinine, how insipid his words sounded?

"Shit," I said to him.

"No," he said. "You think about it for a minute."

I thought about Mr. Semple at my wedding. *You ever*

sleep with my daughter? You ever sleep with my wife? You want to sleep with her?

"You're a pretentious bastard," I said, or something like it.

He had put his pants on and now sat putting on his socks.

"You're a joke, Adams. What you mean is I'm bombastic. *You're* pretentious. . . . I'll tell you something else, OK? I got your ass backed into a corner. The worse thing you could do right now would be to take a swing at me. Oh, yeah, you might knock my ass cold, but that'd only put you in deeper shit with your wife than you're in already. You know it, too, buddy. You know it."

He looked at the floor while he clomped both shoes with his feet in them. But when he looked back up at me his face had changed again. Whatever triumph and viciousness I had read in it a moment ago had been replaced by an expression of unnerving solicitude and fellowship. He swallowed.

"Look, Adams, I'm not so different from you. You ever think of that? I don't hate you and you don't hate me. Yeah, you think you're circumspect and cool, you think you can manipulate me, use me as a straight man, but you don't, you know. The only person you're making a fool of is yourself. Your wife knows that. Everyone in the hotel knows it."

I felt a great ungovernable tide of rage sweeping over me, a tide of rage but also of outrage. The gall, the presumption, the wrongness of what he was saying!

"My wife," I said. "And what's this Mistress Quickly crap?"

"Not what you think, boy. We get along fine to-gether, by the way, while you labor away in your library in London — which I doubt, incidentally."

I started to answer him but he cut me off with a sharp slicing gesture. "People say you're an ass, Adams. But I don't think you are. I think that inside that hard stocky man there's a very unsteady little man, probably a cod-dled Mama's boy, a little creature of the great pampered Eastern Establishment. And not, to judge from appear-ances and what I know about you, a very successful one at that. I understand you couldn't cut it as a teacher."

"Who told you that?"

"One of your kids, maybe."

"The great pampered Eastern Establishment. Pull your head out."

"The great pampered, liberal, Eastern Establishment."

"I don't give a flying fuck for politics."

"You don't give a damn about anything, Adams."

"Neither do you." How childish it was becoming.

"It's more than politics, anyway. You know that wop that ran for Mayor of New York?"

This talk, I imagined, was his way of winding down the little war: discuss stereotypes instead of persons: Marjorie, me, himself. I asked him whether he meant La Guardia or Procaccino, or Impelliteri.

"The middle one, you know who I mean. The one that lost to your hee-ro Lindsay. He coined a good phrase, that wop did, or his ghostwriters. Limousine liberalism. That's your life, boy. Think you're cultured people, elitists, humanitarians, sneer at the rest of the country. Have frenzies of outrage about big issues. Some clown guns down Martin Luther King or Malcolm X and you run around condemning everyone but yourselves, run around raising committees, getting Brinkley to raise his eyebrows on NBC, holding memorial services. Etcetera. But none of you really gives a good goddamn, any more than you do about your kids or your wife."

"You should talk, Freddie."

"I *should* talk. I been where you're headed. I'm old enough to be your father."

"You said that. Don't say it again, either."

He ignored me and went ahead. "But we're no different. Your suits are cut differently and you went to the Ivy League. Maybe you don't drink as much as me, but you will. You come to Lawnsmere for the same reasons I do. The only difference between you and me is that I say the things you're thinking, right out."

"And do the things I'm thinking, too, don't you?"

He was almost fully dressed. He walked over to the wardrobe and reached in for a coat.

"Given the chance, I probably would."

"She'll never give you the chance."

"What makes you think she hasn't already?"

"I know my Marjorie."

"Yeah," he said, "sure you do. Help me on with this thing." He gave me his jacket to hold and he backed his arms into its sleeves. "I had it made special."

32

Frederick Giles was not a violent man, but he was an extraordinarily aggressive and competitive soul.

At this point I didn't care why he was like this. I

vaguely accounted for his personality — his boorishness, his insensate competitiveness, his predisposition to treat everything that affected him as a prospective threat, and, yes, even his unexpected kindnesses and his terrible undisguised preoccupation with what the world thought of him — as the product of "insecurity," and let it go at that. It used to be the fashion to say that we were wasting too much time wondering why we had involved ourselves in Vienam: why look for the arsonist when he's burning the house to the ground? His motives no longer matter. Perhaps my own reasoning in Lawnsmere was as specious as this, but there it was. It was what Giles *did*, not what he was, that I had to worry about.

In war the moral is to the material (according to Napoleon) as three are to one. Giles's advantages were therefore tremendous. He had accurately gauged the state of my marriage; had with devilish accuracy sensed what I was doing in London; and had spent the larger part of my conversations with him railing against the social milieus in which Marjorie and I moved, milieus which he had just summed up as the "great pampered liberal Eastern Establishment," and which, moreover, he sensed were almost as repellent to me as they were to him. He was a cocksure assailant; I an embarrassed, diffident defender.

His campaign had two objectives: I was one, and sleeping with Marjorie (to be perfectly blunt) would be, or already was, the fruit of that victory. The other was the great pampered liberal . . . etcetera. He insisted on showing it up for what he thought it to be; but he could win no victory here, for we would go back to it, and accommodate ourselves to it as we had always done and would always do, and we would forget all about him . . .

Some clown guns down Martin Luther King and we have frenzies of outrage.

None greater than in Routledge, and you may as well hear about it. I'm glad Giles wasn't there to watch.

The morning after the shooting — I was in Routledge during a spring vacation from Grierson, and Marjorie had stayed at the school with the children — Father Frank Flanagan, pastor of Our Lady of Lourdes, put through a call to the Reverend Philip Schieder, our Congregationalist minister. Schieder in turn relayed what Flanagan had suggested during the call to the Episcopal Rector of St. James's, Father Kelley with an *e,* an Orange-Irish cleric who described himself as a "Thirty-Nine Article Man out of Williams and ETS."

Now as a rule the three of them had as little to do with each other as possible, Flanagan being a textbook Dominican whose labored heartiness masked deep suspicions about everyone in the town not connected with his own parish, and Schieder being a real ascetic and a scholar, a man given to long harangues on texts taken from the books of Samuel and Job: harangues oriented to men slaying each other for just reasons. Schieder's flock tolerated him between the *New York Times Magazine* and their noontime bullshots, and he was known then, as now, for having dropped William Styron's baby during a baptismal service.

Finally Kelley: bluff, peppery, husky and crewcut, a man who ate Routledge with a silver spoon, whose favorite approbative outburst was "simply marvelous!";

who was given to Langrock jackets of loose fit and impeccable texture, lined in paisley; who under these invariably sported a paling silk magenta torsoshirt suggesting some future coveted eminence. He had moved smartly into the Vietnam era with a turquoise pectoral cross and the last new Austin-Healey to be legally marketed in the state of Connecticut. I cannot think of him without remembering his two favorite hymns: "I Sing a Song of the Saints of God," and "Once to Every Man and Nation" — the latter a stately portentous anthem which often served as his recessional. By the light of burning martyrs the Routledgians trudge to their country squires.

But a tolerable enough gent who — he told Schieder — quite concurred in Flanagan's "truly inspired idea" that an ecumenical service in honor of Dr. King be held forthwith.

The three of them worked it out, and the service went off two nights later. I got there late and parked across the street from St. James's.

It was a bitterly cold night for April, very clear and damp, cold enough for the exhausts of the cars of the late arrivals to curl upwards in grayish stools and for a little circlet of chauffeurs (*everyone* had come) to have to stamp their feet and beat their fists together. Halfway up the flagstone walk I began to notice, looking towards the great translucent sheet of Otto Kairne windows that were the façade of the church, that the great brown mass of human backs inside was swaying. And as my eyes adjusted to the dark I distinguished lines of heads above the serried ranks of mourners, each succeeding rank shifting in unison from right to left, and back, and again. When I got into the foyer of St. James's I realized what was being done: in a deep Slavic moan the citizens of Routledge were singing Doctor King's song, their arms locked together, mink over flannel, pockabooks depending from forearms in the swaying, halting movement of the mass. Timid phlegmy soprano voices and strong basso profundos, uncertain of the words and therefore weak in the attack, were attempting Doctor King's song. And above the determined flock I could see the face of Kelley behind his pulpit, lit up by his reading lamp, the face of an adult cherub utterly in his element: a face serene and happy and assured — this ecumenical stuff being, in his own words, a real piece of cake.

In the ghostly flicker of candlelight I could see the parishoners' lips form the words of the songs, two of the anthems of the late sixties which had been woven together by some dizzy librettist in the Ladies' Guild.

The words embodied a plea. The Routledgians were asking that peace be given a chance. This was all they were asking, and what could be more simple than that? And if their wish were vouchsafed by the power to whom they addressed themselves, why then they would surely overcome. Indeed they would overcome. We shall oh-ver-cuh-um, oh, oh-ver-ah-cuhm.

I thought of the popular ballad "Who Wears Short Shorts?" Like it, this song had no second verse, no clever reprise. Simply, the citizens of Routledge, Connecticut, were giving notice that they would overcome.

There was a sudden pall of silence followed by a standing prayer in solemn cadence. Again the wish was expressed that peace be given a chance. Then they would overcome, these attorneys and bankers and doctors and coupon cutters and manufacturers, their wives and their

children. Mr. Burdenall, for example, was going to over-
come when he returned from his meeting with Gaylord
Martin down in Philadelphia. Do not doubt that Mr.
Simmons would overcome after he left his mistress next
Thursday on East Seventy-second Street; or that Mrs.
Findon would overcome after she had competed in
Brookline in the Senior Amateurs; or that Dr. and Mrs.
Nettlework would overcome after they paid for the
dormitory at Middlesex School their son Grigor had
burnt to the ground; or that Mrs. Aclaine would over-
come, in her own lovely way, from her veranda at Hobe
Sound. They were all of them determined that peace be
given a chance and that there be no more hate or killing
in the Western, or any world. *Écrasez l'infame!*

Just now they and their friends and children were set-
tling themselves into pews, demurely arranging their
fannies, getting comfortable for what might be a longish
harangue. The men folded their arms across their chests
and struck attitudes of languid benignancy, and their
wives and daughters minced out their last whispers.
Father Kelley introduced Father Flanagan, who came
forward to the pulpit and gingerly massaged the good
Episcopal mahogany, mumbled something indistinguish-
able from the last embarrassed rustlings and coughings,
and looked forward and up to the great chandelier
hanging over us.

"God the Father, God the Son, and God the Hully
Ghost. Amen.

"Some years ago," he began, "when I was only a young
lad, I spent part of a summer in Tuckshorn, Georgia. It
was 1946 and around the time of the Fourth of July, the
day commemorating the founding of this country. I

went out to the Main Street they have there with two of my cousins and watched a parade.

"Now in Georgia they have parades very much like yours and mine. First would come the mayor, or first selectman I think they call it, then the police on their motorcycles, then the Cubs and Brownies, the local beauty queen, high school marching bands, and what not. Near the end of the line of march came a contingent of citizens of the town who had fought in World War II, about fifty or so of them as I recollect. Now among these fifty were about ten black citizens. None of these having been officers, and for the more obvious reasons, they marched at the end of the parade.

"As they passed in front of us I heard a voice yell 'Barracuda Battalion — black backs and yella bellies! They'll run every time!' The voice came from a place that couldn't of been farther than twenty feet from the black veterans. Every one of those negroes heard it. But none of them did anything. They just kept marching along. Like the famous river, they kept rolling along.

"I turned around and looked in the direction the shout had come from. And standing on the corner behind me was a uniformed sheriff reminiscent of what you see in those Dodge car commercials on TV. This sheriff had yelled this thing out at the negro veterans. The man standing next to me looked over at him and shook his head back and forth sadly and maybe a little condescendingly at the sheriff.

"'Commere, nigger lover,' the sheriff said to him. 'I said, Commere.' And then an amazing thing happened, this quiet gentleman that had shook his head at the sheriff went up to him and spat in his face."

Father Flanagan paused, and we waited on tenterhooks for more. But the story, improbable from the beginning, had run its course. I had visions of the young Catholic Flanagan pummeling the sheriff on the thighs and later being branded with a harp and thrown, torn and bleeding, onto a Phoebe Snow Boxcar headed north; also that from the tale he would draw certain inferences for us about the intolerance and hatred of men generally, but especially of men in the American South.

But I was wrong. Flanagan continued: "Now just what is the point of this story? It's just this, I think. That *that* kind of behavior is exactly what we *don't* need, hatred on both sides. A rooted prejudice against the black people made that sheriff yell out what he did, but the man standing next to me should no more have gone up to the sheriff and spat at him than the sheriff should have abused the blacks. For prejudice and hatred are not prisoners of time or station or individuals. They are all pervasive. They must be stamped out. And, as we have been singing this sad evening, overcome. Let us pray."

We prayed, perhaps a little chastened, and we exited slowly after singing "Ye Watchers and Ye Holy Ones." We shook hands with Flanagan, Schieder and Kelley on the steps of the church. We thanked them for what they had done in bringing us together. Among the comments I heard, the following three seem worth recording:

"What other American besides King got the Nobel for Literature?"

"What'd they do to the guy that spat in the sheriff's face?"

"Is Betsy home from Westover?"

33

It had begun to snow, a dry fine dust falling vertically. At the northern limit of Lawnsmere the bells of St. Jude's chimed hoarsely, a melancholy aggrieved carol of warning and lament. For a moment I caught Giles's face in the light streaming through a window of the pub, a face suddenly softer than it had ever seemed before, a face perfectly relaxed in repose — the face, let us say, of a commander who has given his orders and made his dispositions in the assurance they are utterly right, and who calmly awaits the inevitable success they must yield.

He stood between Marjorie and Carstairs' daughter Deirdre waiting for the car to be brought around; and I noticed how easily, how naturally his hands lay on the shoulders of my children, how my son in his Glengarry and his elegant little coat and leggings turned to look up at him as he felt their touch, how he reached up and lay his fingers on Giles's hand. I felt Marjorie's eyes on me: *See how he is with our children, how gentle he is with them.*

There was some small awkwardness when the car finally pulled up before us. "Where would you be most comfortable?" Giles asked me with mocking solicitude. I got in front next to Carstairs, and Giles and the two women slid into the back seat, Giles between them.

"Where do *you* want to sit?" Giles asked the children.

"With you, Uncle Frederick."

"OK. You sit with your daddy," he told my daughter.
"And you jump in back here with me, young man."

Ten minutes later we arrived at Greylarch.

There are certain sounds which create terror with
devastating suddenness; things like the sound of an enemy mortar being fired from some unknown distance at
night, the kind of sound you actually feel before you
hear it. Most of us are spared such things, though we can
remember or imagine them well enough. One such noise
is no less terrifying for its frequency: a dry rattling
sound which gathers thickly but evenly in volume like a
cylinder of gravel shook slowly, then violently — a
sound that always leads to a bursting hungry expression
of raw lusting viciousness.

You can hardly move when you hear it. And yet you
feel as much anger as terror when you do. It was absolutely black and silent in Orme's driveway; I could feel
the snow but I could not see it. I imagined the noise was
coming from the throat of a wild predator, perhaps one
of those awful German police dogs. I had only a second
to back myself against the side of the car and put my
hands over my face; I sensed the animal was holding his
charge, cruelly savoring his advantage and judging
where to strike, and at that moment I turned long
enough to see the faces of Giles and Marjorie with insane
disfiguring laughter in them, obscene grins, and I saw
her hand on his lap as he leaned forwards and seemed to
point at my legs. I turned back again with my palms on
the car door.

Now a bright yellow light suddenly slanted directly at
our car from an open door thirty feet away, and in it I
saw the outline of a tall male figure walking carefully
towards us in the snow. At the base of the light, on the

ground immediately in front of me, lay a kind of collapsed carpetbag, its sides working like a bellows.

Suddenly a beam of light flashed at my face.

"Is that Mark? Is that Captain Mark Adams? My *dear* fellow, what a handsome surprise! Mark Adams and family. Napier, cease that dreadful racket!"

The carpetbag now showed itself capable of locomotion. It stopped growling, withdrew reluctantly from the attack and moved off haunchily towards its master. This was Napier, Orme Goderich's basset hound.

"Idle dog! House-house-house-house!" The animal adjusted his gait ever so slightly, unconcernedly negotiated the stairs to the porch, and disappeared inside the house.

"My *dear* fellow! What a treat, what a treat." Colonel Goderich backed off and scrutinized me, as generals do when they haven't seen each other in a long time, reaching out finally to shake hands. "Looking very fit, very fit. Bloody beast, not civil to anyone, took him out of a kennel in Huddersfield, rotten Lancashire temperament. My dear fellow, how are you? Get the others out of that wheeled den of nicotine!"

He opened doors and I began introducing them all. "Felix Carstairs, whom you know."

"Yes, yes, Felix, old fellow, and splendid daughter, my dear hahryou? And Marjorie, dear girl, my *droit de jambon* shall be a kiss on the lip, and? . . ."

"This is Mr. Frederick Giles, Orme, all the way from Chicago for your Christmas Eve shindig."

"That's it, that's it, Christmas shin-dig, howyedo? Vehrd much about you, all of it good. Friend of this scoundrel here, eh? Do come inside, warm you up. Son and daughter Adams, welcome! Welcome all!" We followed him into Greylarch.

It was a rough rambling house, a place I can hardly describe adequately, never having seen it before or since. Besides, the evening's activities were confined to five or six rooms only: the downstairs loo; a large drawing room which had been transformed into a kind of dance hall for the occasion; two bedrooms at the head of the stairs leading up from the drawing room; a well-appointed kitchen-pantry; and Colonel Goderich's study, a kind of anteroom, which we entered now.

Before a huge charred fireplace, ringing a dying fire in a semicircle, lay five wicker dogbaskets with Napier in the smallest of them. A black retriever bitch, her head hanging over the tattered edge of an adjoining berth, kept a kind of watch over him, hunching her ears each time he started in his sleep, ignoring both our noisy entrance and the children's excited petting of her. Across the bare floor, set back in a kind of bay, was a huge captain's desk, also very rough and covered with stains and burns, open books and collapsing stacks of letters and papers. Like sentinels on either side of it great bookcases stood against the walls, their shelves extending from floor to ceiling, full of books with titles like *Memoirs of the Peninsula,* by A Sergeant.

A number of wraps and overcoats also lay on the desk, and I saw and began to hear that the planned revels were already in progress in the other rooms of Greylarch: from the tone of things, and from the merry, almost anxious expression on Goderich's face, very well in progress. By the time Marjorie and I got our things off he was already leading the way out of the study with his hand on the back of Giles's arm, and the two of them appeared absorbed in some earnest conversation. On the face of it, they had taken to each other rapidly; and again I heard the phrase "so much about you" as they disappeared into the hall. Goderich said it, not Giles.

There were thirty people in the drawing room. I got Marjorie and myself double vodkas and stood looking at the scene.

Almost without exception the guests had divided themselves by sex. The men, and I noticed our friend Faricy among them, stood in two stiff clumps by the far wall, under a row of four immense portraits of British Army officers. More than half were in uniform, glittering and resplendent in beautifully cut costumes, the colors and facings of which proclaimed their regimental affiliations and the unspoken gradations of their caste. Those few in evening dress, like Faricy, stood confidently among them, as though they too had worn, or were entitled to wear such costumes. In all cases, however, their posture, the way they held their glasses and cigarettes, the inclination of their heads, their slick, immaculately parted hair, the quiet but authoritarian inflections of their voices, the fit of their narrow striped trousers over their densely muscled thighs and calves, the casual stony *coups d'oeil* in which they kept themselves informed of the arrival of newcomers — these things advertised their station in life, their caste, so well, so flagrantly even, that it was as though they were consciously adapting themselves to the accepted caricature of British officers at their ease. The air was quietly thick with their talk, but only certain phrases could be heard from where I stood: "yes, quite's" and "*my dear fellow*'s" and punctilious, accommodating "quite right's" seemed to predominate. If you were as drunk as I became later that night, and if you had not seen these men (but only heard them), you might have sworn you were listening to a group of poor understudies of W. C. Fields. Meanwhile, I had the impression that the civilians were doing most of the talking, and also that they seemed distinctly less consequential than the soldiers.

Giles and Orme Goderich had joined one group of them, and I saw Giles bring his heels together as he was presented to each officer. I saw, too, that Orme kept one hand on Giles's back as he introduced him to the others, and was making expansive motions with his right hand as he presented him, as though Giles himself were a man of great consequence.

We stood drinking near the bar, and I looked at the women. They too were easily classifiable: they had sorted themselves into two groups. One comprised women who looked to be about forty-five or fifty; the others were their daughters, I guessed.

My God, what marvelous dissipation shone in the faces of the older ones! What pampered, lubricious skin stretched softly taut over cheekbone and chin and forehead! Skin greased and oiled nightly in ancient narcissistic ritual, slack carmine lips waxily parted over stained teeth, earlobes pricked and stretched by outsized shining earrings. And yet this dissipation did not seem to extend to their bodies: they were unguently but athletically supple, casually erect, and the placement of their feet — which one could judge even under their long dresses — bespoke lives of riding in county hunts and endless tramping through gorsey moors; a firm-footed, casual competence in domestic and animal things, an indulgent but settled maternity and easy dominance over their sons and daughters. Most of all, their faces and bodies together seemed to bespeak a raw joy in the pleasures of animal sex.

Why soften the judgment? Had you stood there, had you the normal sensibility of a restless American husband, you would surely have come to it yourself. Several years ago there was a terribly messy divorce in Britain involving a duchess said to be a nymphomaniac. One paper called her a "twentieth-century Semiramis," and it alleged as genuine a note she was said to have written one of her lovers. "I have thought of some interesting things we can do," it concluded, "some interesting things we can do." I wondered what this fiery stimulus did to the lover when he received it. Its casual understatement must have driven him wild — especially since he had been doing other "interesting" things with her before: the supply of treats was inexhaustible. And yet only . . . "some interesting things we can do."

The women would be crones in Brighton or Bournemouth in fifteen years, I thought. Their breasts would fall away limp, bated, sagging almost to their hipbones. Their teeth would seem truly to grow longer, their faces more slack-jawed and indulged than ever. They would be perfectly composed at their husbands' early funerals; and already they would be looking anxiously at the faces of the men who mourned him.

But just now their eyes shone as they permitted themselves to be introduced. I remembered the old story that measured them perfectly: a stableboy, holding the bridle of a gentlewoman's horse, noticed and remarked on the exhausted condition of the animal; and she, answering him: "You'd be exhausted too, Simon, had *you* spent five hours between my legs."

Their eyes shone in the warm room. I reached for another drink and watched them come over to introduce their daughters to Carstairs and some other guests who had come in. But in these daughters it was impossible to see any such future course of dissolution. Some were fresh as wildflowers, creamy and plump and succulent in their mothers' old ball gowns; others, more slight, narrow chested and marsupial-looking in languid, hips-forward stances, came up with them to introduce themselves to Marjorie and Deirdre, regarding them and me in frank twinkling stares, putting out their hands like satiny gloves.

And, "How d'ye do, young man?" one of them said to my little son. "Is this your sister? How d'ye do? What're your names? Colonel Orme's grand neph-oo and niece, are you not, come for your gifts? Has Mummy brought them with her?"

"No, Santa Claus," my son said, eyes on her décolletage.

"Ah, Santa Claus. Father Christmas." She unbent herself from his scrutiny and told Marjorie how precious they were, and I told her they would soon be put to bed.

"Don't I get my presents first, Daddy?"

"A little later, sweetheart."

"Don't I?"

"Of course you do, darling," Marjorie reassured her.

"I want to see the puppies."

"Shall I take them out? You look as though you've got plenty to keep you occupied," she said to me.

I told her there was a new litter somewhere downstairs and that then she should take them up.

"Easy on the sauce, Mark." She walked away with her hands on the children's heads. She did not notice the two new guests who passed her, nor did they notice her — since they had already seen me and had never met Marjorie.

It was David Ashley and Margot. Good God, I thought, and I walked over to meet them halfway.

34

You begin to feel your age a little when you're thirty or thirty-five, but only in ways you think about after certain activities. For example, you might sit in a locker room and think that ten years ago you would have gotten to a difficult baseline shot or a drop volley you had missed playing tennis. Or you might wonder that it's taken you so long to memorize a list of figures or dates. Or, badly hungover, you might remember that when you were twenty you could drink all night, take a cold shower and go to work, and work properly. The last consideration has kept me from drinking very much since I left the Army. I never really thought a good therapeutic drunk worth it.

The exception, of course, was tonight. In my powerlessness to stop what I saw was happening to me and what was going on between Giles and Marjorie, I knew the terrible misery that only such impotence entails. In a way it was like watching yourself sucked into a bad wreck, knowing it's too late to arrest the speed of your car or even to swerve to avoid another, and yet being impressed afterwards that the thing seemed to develop as if it *were* developing of its own volition — at a pace of dogged, maddening slowness, rich in eerily sharp detail of which you were grotesquely aware all the while it was happening.

Perhaps I was into my third drink when I walked over to meet Margot and David. In any case I remember well enough David's explanation of how he had traced us to Greylarch. He had got back that afternoon, "from the smog-wretched citadel of the North, Liverpool." He knew we were in a hotel in Lawnsmere and he reckoned we wouldn't be found dead in any hotel but the Rufus — which he had called. They had not answered, so he and Margot had driven there and Susan had told him we were at Colonel Goderich's.

They did hope they were not intruding. But Margot had been so charmed by me that she had insisted — and after all, it wasn't as though they were going to see us every month. Soon we would be back in America, wouldn't we? And they had never met Marjorie.

Solemnly, and with some little ceremony, David curled his lips into the finest smirk I've ever seen. We embraced like Italians and I kissed Margot on the cheek.

Orme had seen them come in. He detached himself from Giles and his guests and walked over quickly, stretching out his hand to Margot. He looked at me without saying anything, and I introduced them.

"Quite possibly *need* a doctor before the night's out, what?"

"I don't know about this one, Orme," I told him.

"Why not?" he demanded.

"He's not a good man to set working on women," I explained.

Orme forced a thin smile. "Likely that mass of decrepit soldiery'll need him, not these women my dear hahyrou?" With no break in his host's patter — he had mastered the art of breathing in the middle, not at the end, of his sentences — Orme moved smoothly away from us and began talking to the girl my son had admired earlier.

"Not happy about our being here, it appears."

I told David I was sure Orme didn't mind.

But I was certain Orme had been put off by their intrusion into his annual Christmas party. Conceivably — if Margot had looked like anything but what she so obviously was — he would not have minded; but he did mind. His sense of good form had been offended. Perhaps also he had calculated too precisely the number of guests he had invited; perhaps he had worked out how much they would eat and drink and laid in just enough. He was a hospitable, thoroughly ingratiating man, but he was one of those people who could brook no amendment of his plans. Everything had to be in good order. Once back at Grierson during his visit I had watched him level off all the picture frames in my study. Embarrassed when he turned to look at me, he had passed it off as the rebellion of what he called a covertly artistic personality against a remembered military discipline. The Germans, it seemed, had had a pleasant habit of nudging pictures out of alignment, hoping the British officers would straighten them when they occupied the quarters the Germans abandoned in their retreat across North Africa. The crooked pictures were all booby-trapped. Vaguely too I wondered if some remark of Marjorie's had stimulated his suspicions: had she said to him something like "Mark's off gallivanting around in London . . ."

Well, it couldn't be helped. We went over to some dining room chairs Orme had set about the edge of the dance floor and sat down.

About this time as I remember it the music began, or

maybe resumed, a grating fox-trot scratched with a blunt needle off an old 78 record. Reluctantly the men abandoned their conversations and moved towards their wives and daughters — led, as they walked towards them, by one of the very few men there who had no wife or daughter or date with him, Frederick Giles. I watched him go up to one of the older women, execute a perfect snapping little bow — one hand flat across his stomach, the other against the small of his back — extend his hand to her, and lead her out to dance.

What a pisser, I thought. But however ridiculous the bow might have been, I had to admit he danced well; not well, in fact, but beautifully. Somehow I had envisioned him awkwardly executing a pumping, jerky box-step with his eyes on his feet, as though he had been to Arthur Murray's in Winnebago Terrace to take a cram course for his visit. But no. Where he had seemed obtuse and even lumpy in the pub, locked in his earnest monologues over the Nelson Table, clomping around the room in his shower clogs, even in the snow outside the Rufus Arms, he now seemed transformed into a kind of courtier: a youngish, accommodating roué. His movements were gracefully, offhandedly inventive; his patter was drawing warm smiles from his partner. I even thought his eyes gleamed with happy malevolence as successive spins and twirls brought his face into view.

Now he was moving, he and his lady, among the other couples, negotiating his way among them with unerring, unbumping facility. So fluently did they move over the floor that the others were beginning to notice him, and I noticed myself that two of the women were drawing the attention of their own stiff partners to Giles and his.

"You seem absorbed, Mark."

I said I wasn't absorbed, only tired and a little drunk.

"I shouldn't wonder."

"I suppose you shouldn't," I said, and at the same time I felt Margot's fingers coldly insinuating themselves into the palm of my hand.

"A good time was had by all, I understand, in my absence," said David.

"A fair statement, wouldn't you say so, Mark?"

I agreed with her, wondering how much she had told him, and I despised her. I must have communicated my wretchedness, too. Though I was vaguely conscious of my obligation to make them feel welcome after Orme's chilly reaction, and though I wanted to sound and look offhanded about the thing, I could not, and David saw this.

"Mark, Mark! Old friends. Vegetable act."

"Right, David, vegetable act."

"So for god's sake don't be awkward about it. Margot doesn't care."

"Shall we dance?" Margot asked me.

I told her not just yet. I wanted terribly to be alone, to drink and sleep and be alone and let things take their course.

"Where's your wife?"

I said that she had taken the children to see Goderich's new litter of Norwich terrier puppies, and I asked them to behave themselves when she returned. They were both quite tight. David's eyes had that zany, rakish expression in them that portended all kinds of indiscretions.

Marjorie was walking towards us now, without the children. The kennel must have been out behind the main house, for her face shone brightly pink and there were flecks of snow in her hair. There was something exotically magisterial about her tonight, a compound of *gaminerie* and an almost gleeful self-assurance in her stride, in the way she looked down at me as she came towards us, something even of Giles's smirking, unbearable arrogance.

With David she was routinely cordial. But she treated Margot as though she were my mother and Margot some unlovely, unexpected blind date of her son's. She appraised her coolly: Here, she was thinking, is what my husband used to chase after, in Cambridge that year when he was writing me those pathetic letters and I wasn't answering them. She looked from Margot to me and then to David, and she asked him to dance with her.

"Do give old Margot a whirl," David called over his shoulder.

And so we all danced together now: Frederick Giles weaving his inventive, salamandrine patterns among and around the sedate English couples and their artless young daughters and their shy escorts, charming his partner as thoroughly as he must have charmed Marjorie when I was not with them; David Ashley, allowing himself to be led by Marjorie; and I with my eager repulsive bedmate of the day before.

Giles waited only a minute or two before doublecutting with David and Marjorie. About this time the music changed to some Latin rhythm, an arrangement of an old song I used to call "To You My Heart Cries Out Forsythia." In a confident *schuss* Giles twirled Marjorie away from David, and they glided off towards the great paintings at the end of the room, spinning in a pinwheeling efflorescence until they had distanced themselves enough from the rest of us. Now she lay her temple against his jaw and her eyes closed, and I saw them raise their clasped hands close to their faces and finally I saw Giles take Marjorie in his arms and with his hands folded at the small of her back whisper to her . . .

"That's an American with your wife now?"

"Yes, Margot," I told her, "an old friend of ours from the Midwest."

But I could no longer deny my fatigue and perhaps my drunkenness. Suddenly I felt I might collapse if I stayed any longer with her. I was beginning to lurch and trip and lean on her as we swayed idly together, and I made some sort of apology to her and bolted away to Orme's study.

35

I drank from a bottle of Irish whiskey I found on Orme's desk and lay for a long time on a leather sofa next to it. Giles is unalloyed gall, I thought. Gall is when you take a healthy, as we used to call it, on someone's doorstep, and then knock and ask for toilet paper. Gall is when you go after someone's wife when you know any reaction from her husband will only strengthen your case. Gall . . . I listened to the slowly rising wash, the gathering clink and stomp and hiss of the party down the long hallway, and I thought how splendidly dramatic it all was; what antic impulses and energies had gone to the creation of my terrible predicament, how sharply and uncontrollably it all seemed to be happening. The heat and the gathering tumult of the party, its fra-

grances and its repressed desires and the silent lusts of
the women and officers and local guests were somehow
more redolent, more palpable here among Orme's dogs
and books and memorabilia than they had been in his
drawing room. I could feel and hear the rhythms of the
dancing change again, yielding now suddenly to the
madcap beat of the Charleston. I imagined Marjorie
kicking off her pumps and joyously preening herself in
her self-conscious mastery of its foolish rubbery gyra-
tions, that stupid thing you do with your hands on your
knees while you pretend to look at your partner; and
the floor was being cleared for them and the English
were urging them into it, watching Marjorie all the
time while Giles like a confident picador aped her
motions but kept his distance, effacing his presence just
enough that they would all watch her only and envy
him, just aware that he hovered at the edge of the floor,
ready to reclaim her in a triumphant adulatory embrace
when she finished . . .

Someone shouted, "Scotch Foursomes!" and the house
rumbled as they shuffled for position. A breathless
adolescent voice was shouting directions, and there was
sharp girlish laughter.

Each time I brought the bottle to my lips the dogs, all
of them now in their baskets, lifted their heads and
looked vacantly at me and then sometimes after doing
this they looked back at each other. Then resignedly
their heads would drop and they would lie on their chins.

It was meaningless, I was thinking, whatever Giles
and Marjorie were doing. I no longer had any control.
Perhaps Margot was telling Marjorie how "good" I was;
or perhaps Giles and Marjorie were kissing open-
mouthed on the dance floor; perhaps Orme's haughty

guests, his pendulous women and their curt husbands were beginning to cleave to other partners and perform the mincing sexual parodies of dances they had half learned watching their own children.

Giles would do what he wanted with her, and she would do what she wanted with him. She would forget if she had not already forgotten those evenings in which he had sat spouting his arrant unwisdom, the facts and opinions he had culled from book jackets and anthologies left in his room. And then, after a decent interval, she would remember all this again; and she would take her vengeance on him as she had on me. I drank again and the bottle dropped to the rug and I felt myself sliding into sleep as though I were slipping irretrievably down an icy, endless, toboggan slide. The music, I remember, seemed to throb inside me like a hungry tumor; but I was escaping from it, from the welter of heat and the eerie siena-orange light of the dying fire, escaping into a terrible silence, sustained and premonitory, but pure with the cast of silver and blue.

Later I was able to remember that people had looked in on me, and that a man said "poor bugger"; and I had an idea also that children scuttled upstairs like ferrets and that from some source above me there was radiant caroling and laughter. Earnest pink boys in cassocks were singing of the snow that lay round about firm and crisp and even, and couples strolled dreamily up and down the hall, and stairs creaked. I dreamed I was awake and shouting for it all to stop and pulling at him and noticing he was the only man there not in evening clothes and that he was at her with his coat on; and that she looked up at me with the same hideously mocking expression she had forced when the dog went after me outside the car, and that Giles's head turned full around and looked up at me while he did, and that his face gaped like the face of a fish.

"Your wife, old boy. Hweah's your wife?"

Goderich stared down at me. He was standing planted between my feet like Mr. Semple at my wedding. My hips had slid down over the edge of the sofa and my legs felt like a million atoms and ants tumbling. Only the fire and the stirring of the dogs at their master's presence and the plangent sound of a plucked double bass, far less insistent and noisy than before, restored me to consciousness of where I was, and had been. I looked up at the pallid blur defining itself into Orme's face. I remember thinking that his mustache looked like a chevron.

I asked him what time it was and he told me almost two-thirty.

"I don't know where they are," I told him. I had been asleep more than two hours. I had not been there to give the children their presents. I had not watched the King's choir on BBC-1. The windows at the door of the study were webbed in a powdery filigree of snow and the wind was howling outside. Perhaps David and Margot had left.

"Your children are asleep upstairs. They've had their gifts."

He spoke so well, you could hear him say the *t* in gifts.

I asked him how the party was.

Orme turned sideways and toed at the fire. "About the same condition as the fiuh," he said. "You know how these things progress."

"I should go up and get Marjorie."

"Makes you think she's upstairs? The loo's down here. Had a bit of a doze, have you?"

"She's probably upstairs."

"Talked to your friend from Chicago. Nice chap, that. Did well in the war."

I got up from the sofa and walked down the hall towards the entrance to the stairway, turning before I went up to look at the drawing room. A musty brown light from a chandelier etched a scene like a fraternity house cellar. Flaccid music seemed to coil slowly through it like cigar smoke, and along the walls, in love seats and sofas, the English officers and their wives lay or sat stretched together. The tunics of some of the officers had been undone at the collar, in some cases removed to show them bird-chested in sleeveless undershirts. Only David and Margot sat upright, and they were talking animatedly to each other.

I walked up the stairs and opened the first door to the left.

The light from the hall shone in on them, on my son over by the far wall, balled up in sleep with his face at the bars of his crib and with his bangs plastered over his forehead and his mouth open, and on Marjorie and Frederick Giles lying together, uncovered and fully clothed, on Goderich's enormous canopied bed. One of Giles's hands lay cupped under his head and a cigarette drooped from his lips. Marjorie lay at his side in a sort of contrived supine sprawl, her legs together and tipped to one side like the fin of a mermaid.

"Hello, there, scholar," he said. Deliberately, so as not to wake Marjorie, he slipped his hand out from under his head and took the cigarette from his mouth. He flicked the ash to the floor.

"With my son in the room?" I said to him. "Too much, Freddie, too much."

"Too much what?" he said.

I told him not to play any of his fucking games with me and that Marjorie's father was a Jew.

One of Marjorie's feet moved, and I noticed her dancing pumps were still on. Her hand moved over his chest, but she still seemed asleep.

"Tell her I'll be in London with David Ashley when she gets you out of her system, which won't be long."

Still he did not answer, so I left them and went into the next bedroom to kiss my daughter and pull the comforter up around her shoulders. And when I walked back down the upstairs hall I heard Marjorie talking to Giles in a perfectly composed interrogative tone, "What did he say?" and then, a second or two later, "That's rich." Several minutes later I left Greylarch with David and Margot.

36

There's nothing much more to tell. I stayed in London with Margot and David and did not call the Rufus Arms, though I did send Carstairs enough money to pay for my family's expenses for another week. I finished what little research I had left to do for my life of Sir Gordon Sandstone — which, incidentally, I have never written — concluding that the General and Orme would have admired each other very much. Neither David nor Margot pressed me on my arrangements or on what I intended doing when I got back to America; nor did they seem willing to join in my speculations about whether Giles and Marjorie had actually slept together the night of Orme's party or any other time. Very early on the morning my return ticket said we were due to fly home, I walked in a cold and steeping fog from David's flat as far as Hyde Park Corner. Briefly I imagined Frederick Giles on the speaker's platform there haranguing a mob of bemused Englishmen on the demiurges of world-historical forces and the literature of Ernie Pyle. Then I got into a cab and drove to the airport.

I waited in the lounge about twenty minutes and read the Paris edition of the *Herald Tribune*. The Los Angeles Lakers had just won their thirtieth game in a row. American warplanes continued to hammer the Laotian Panhandle. Dr. Leary was thought to have left Algiers for Afghanistan. I took a sip of orange juice and put the glass in front of me on the table.

A hand reached across my shoulder and held a tiny gin bottle over the glass. "Pour?" said Marjorie.

"Nothengiew."

"Hello, Big One," she said.

I kissed her and told her how classy she looked.

"My classy education did that."

"Got everything out of your system?"

"I suppose. Had a good wash or two?"

The children stood knobby-kneed next to the table. My daughter was twirling a BOAC bag over her head like a lariat. Marjorie sat down next to me.

"No questions," she said. "Not now or ever."

"Anything you say," I told her.

"Kiss your children. They've missed you."

There was some jarring turbulence over Labrador and after one buffeting, sideways jolt Marjorie reached for my hand and put her head on my shoulder. "Maybe I didn't do what you think I did."

"Maybe you did," I said. "Probably you did."

"You too, probably. Vegetable act for a man, though, right?"

Going through customs the inspecting officer looked up from Marjorie's suitcase. "Those are great-looking kids," he said, pointing at our children. I thanked him for the compliment. Usually airport people in those jobs seem resentful and officious.

The man asked what the children's names were, and I told him: Mark and Marjorie.

"High-class name you got there, Babe Ruth," he said to my son. "Who you named after?"

They're named for their parents, I told him . . .